The Golden Ass

The Golden Ass

(an entertainment)

Ciaran O'Driscoll

First published in Ireland by

The Limerick Writers' Centre
c/o The Umbrella Project, 78 O'Connell St., Limerick

www.limerickwriterscentre.com
www.facebook.com/limerickwriterscentre

Book Design: Lotte Bender
Cover Image: from Screenprint by Sioban Piercy
Managing Editor LWC: Dominic Taylor

ISBN 978-1-7384997-1-7

Available as an e-book at www.smashwords.com/limerickwriterscentre
Print copy: www.limerickwriterscentre.com

ACIP catalogue number for this publication is available from The British Library

 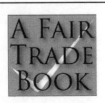 

To John Davies, who gave this novel a head of steam through our earlier collaborative engagement.

CRITICS ON CIARAN O'DRISCOLL'S LIFE-WRITING AND FICTION

A Runner Among Falling Leaves (Childhood Memoir)

I grew up in the town of this memoir. It all comes back to me through O'Driscoll's poetic eye, the back row of Egan's cinema, the stink and sweat of Fair Days, the schoolboy jingles, the girls swimming in the King's River... a deeply affecting, traumatic relationship between father and son.

– Thomas Kilroy, author of The Big Chapel

The book combines nostalgia with truth and social commentary with poetry.... O'Driscoll's return to his background and his humane portrayal of growing up, a process which is life-long, is rich and compelling.

– Sue O'Connor, The Reader (UK)

At a time when we risk losing the run of ourselves in the forever 'new' Ireland of today, this brave, honest book should not be missed.'

– Gerald Dawe, The Irish Times

A Year's Midnight (Novel)

Ghost story, travelogue, existentialist tale of love and detailed exploration of the psyche all rolled into one.

– Billy O'Callaghan, The Irish Examiner

I found *A Year's Midnight* by Ciaran O'Driscoll extremely funny but also enjoyed the surreal inventiveness, and the way he uses landscape and animals (the dogs alone ought to make this book a best seller), mystery and the uncovering of secrets.

– Susanna Jones, author of The Missing Person's Guide to Love

A Year's Midnight is a wonderful and beautiful piece of work – written by someone who has the eye of a painter, the ear of a listener and the pen of a poet. A book that entwines sensual delight with wry humour, landscape with lunacy a joy from first to last.

– John MacKenna, author of The Space Between Us

CONTENTS

1

Martin Goes To Friesland

Martin was married with three children, living in a house in a Parisian suburb, a teacher with a small network of friends and colleagues, and a few students who actually admired him. He had recurrent dreams and memories of being a monk. In one of these memories, he was wearing a long religious habit and over it an RAF greatcoat which was as long as the habit, and he was walking to the bus that would take him back to his friary on the Left Bank, carrying a bag in which two large bottles of a famous liqueur clinked together.

The greatcoat and the clinking bottles were given to him by the wife of the manufacturer of the liqueur. 'Did your mother send you over here without a coat?' she joked. She had been in the Resistance.

He remembered the Eiffel Tower as being to his left that day, the early morning boulevard, wide and with few people, the overcast sky, the first shoots of leaves on the trees, the cold breeze, the cupolas on roof-corners of ornately uniform buildings.

Whenever he thought about it, he had to admit that he had entered the Zone of Renunciation willingly and with the enthusiasm of personal revelation: not quite Paul struck from his horse on the road to Damascus, but with a joy which was undeniable and liberating. And his novice master, in his first year of enclosure, had mapped the journey he was about to undertake. It would not be all light, again and again the darkness would descend: there were several stages on the Mystical Way. But when the darkness descended, and stayed for longer than seemed to him reasonable, Martin began to have doubts about the authenticity of the enterprise (even though his novice master had warned that the darkness would take the form of this very doubting).

Along came a young woman for good measure. And the Mystic Zone's very existence was disproved: it was a form of social control, to divert some of the most energetic and intelligent people from the struggle against the oppressions of Capitalist Society.

At present he was in a place called Sexbierum, in the Dutch Province of Friesland. The very name was enough to evoke the Halfway Place: sex and beer were what had put paid to his vocation. Ostensibly, he was in Sexbierum to do research on the Dutch Admiral Tjerk Hiddes de Vries, and was staying in a pensione run by a rather snooty couple who bred Irish Setters, in a reputedly puritan belt of the Netherlands. Not exactly the place for sex, beer and rum.

He had been a chaplain in a psychiatric hospital just before he left the monks. After mass, it was traditional for the priest to call over to the nurses' quarters for a cup of tea. He got on jokey and eventually flirty terms with a young student nurse who was frequently on desk duty there whenever he came. It led to a couple of secret assignments: courting sessions in secret places such as his brother's empty apartment, or in the dark of cinemas to which he would arrive in mufti. He was smitten, but she wasn't all that smitten. He said he would leave the monks, but her Catholic conscience wouldn't allow her to be the cause of that. He left anyway.

He sat pondering these memories in the pleasant morning sunshine, in the shade of the veranda, and didn't want to do anything else. A friend of his in Paris had recommended that he visit more trendy parts of Friesland, such as Harlingen, or even cross over the Friesian border and visit the theatrical city of Groningen, but he hadn't the slightest desire to go anywhere. He let his mind wander inanely. *Groningen in Groningen, no sooner said than gone again. Yo-ho-ho and a bottle of rum, here I be in*

Sexbierum. The same Parisian friend had told him that young people in that part of Holland, rebelling against the Puritanism, had stolen road signs for Sexbierum and posted them up at the entrances to their parties, with slashes inserted thus in the word – SEX/BIER/RUM. But for him there might be beer and rum from the local off-licence, *but certainly no sex* (said his Conscience).

On the bench beside him, he had a notebook and a weighty tome relating to the seventeenth-century history of Holland. He had bought these in Amsterdam as a camouflage for his idleness. It had worked with his landlady: she didn't see anything wrong with a scholar staying around all day, and even offered him the uncustomary status of full board, which he gladly accepted.

Martin had been having regular dreams at home of being sexually abused by an incubus in his sleep and it was becoming embarrassing for two reasons: firstly because he was enjoying the sex – on one occasion he had even said 'Thank you' to the incubus when it seemed to roll off him and lie in the bed between him and Sarah, his wife; and secondly because Sarah had overheard his moans of pleasure from time to time. The whole experience convinced him that he was transitioning, under the influence of the incubus, from a conventional male in terms of sexuality, to being passively gay, and he had sensed with alarm that this transition might only be the beginning of a roller-coaster of sexual identities, and also that his one identifiable incubus might be joined by many more if he continued on this alarming trajectory.

His reaction, he acknowledged to himself, had been that of Flight, but he was relieved to find that his first two nights, spent in Amsterdam, had been free of ghostly sexual visitors, as had his first night in Friesland, from which he was not long awake.

The morning proceeded pleasantly, and he was just about to commence his midday prayers when the landlady appeared with some lunch: split pea soup and bread.

'You know the work of the mind also can make hungry,' she said and smiled. She seemed to have taken to him.

2

ADRI

Martin had brought another book with him to Friesland which he was actually reading. It was an Irish autobiography called *The Hungarian for Cheese* written by one Adrian Gifford, who was not highly regarded at home but sold well in the UK. Its title was derived from the author's memory of one suppertime in his boarding school, when two refugee boys from the Hungarian Uprising of 1956 were asked what was their word for cheese, little foil-covered Galtee triangles of which lay on their plates, along with pats of butter. The response caused an outburst of hilarity in the refectory: the Hungarian for cheese was SHOYT.

Martin was reading this memoir surreptitiously, making sure that Mrs de Yong didn't catch him abandoning his study of Admiral de Vries. That morning he was gripped by a passage concerning the molestation of the author by a senior boy.

It happened one day in May. I was sitting alone on the grass of the playing field, behind the goal posts, togged out in my shorts and jersey, bored and langorous, zonked by the heat. Fr Bosco, the sports coach, was late. Some of the boys were warming up in anticipation of a practice match, but most of them were sitting around aimlessly, like me.

Suddenly a senior boy came up and sat beside me. 'I'm going to show you what to do with a girl when you take her to the pictures', he announced. His hand was already halfway up my jersey. It roved up and down my belly, raising a tingle like static on my skin. He cupped my 'breasts' and played with my nipples, moved down again towards my genitals, bringing on a shock of embarrassment and transgression, a fearful fascination with such a violating kind of touch, a drift towards compliance with such strange attentiveness and interest in my body. Because boy was I hungry for attention in that place of punishing asceticism – any kind of attention, but especially from a senior boy!

The passage hit him with such vividness that it seemed like an actual memory, and perhaps it had provoked one. He had been very athletic as a fifteen-year-old, the sports trainer had called him a 'great little runner', and he must have been very lithe and lissom and physically attractive in those days. And now he found himself fantasizing about being touched up by a senior boy named Scanlon in his own boarding school – and where was that name coming from? He went on to speculate about how the relationship with Scanlon might have developed, and places in the college which might have been suitable for trysting in – the toilet or some unused room. And how he and Scanlon might have been caught by the dean of discipline having sex in the music room.

Scanlon, of course, had chosen him rather than any other junior boy because he was the most alluring of all the junior boys who were slumped lazily on the playing field under the afternoon sun of May…

He took a nap after lunch in an armchair and woke with a start to find that a red setter was on top of him, humping his exposed thigh. He jumped and the setter bolted through the open bedroom door. The humping had brought on an orgasm, but there was no stickiness: an orgasm of the mind. He wondered was the incubus back to abuse him through the proxy form of a dog. The thought was enough to send him by taxi to the nearest hostelry, for a stiff drink or two.

Two men in vests were playing billiards in the tavern, and there was also a couple with a baby, who was sleeping in a buggy. The couple were watching the players and talking together in low voices. Martin seemed to recognize Irish accents. There was no one else there except the barmaid, a woman in middle age, who recommended Oude Genever to Martin when he asked for a stiff drink.

'Ah yes. Strong drink. We have Oude Genever. Yes?'

'Yes', Martin said, and perhaps it was the innocence of the sleeping baby that brought its opposite to Martin's mind, but he was struck by a memory from his university days in London – his philosophy tutor quoting the Latin adage, *Corruptio Optimi pessima*. The corruption of the best is the worst. Martin now realized, for the very first time, here in Friesland, at the age of forty, that the tutor who had quoted the Latin adage to him when he was a thirty-year-old just out of the cloister, was not trying to impress him with his learning, but suggesting that he, Martin, could progress from saintly innocence to rampant *homme-fatal* sex under the tutelage of his university mentor. Something began to stir in him that called for more Oude Genever to quell it, and to stop him eyeing the big man in the string vest.

The other Irishman had begun a stop-start conversation with the big billiard player, which consisted mainly of enthusiasms and agreements with enthusiasms.

'He beautiful baby, very beautiful. He sleep.'

'Oh yes. He's a very good sleeper.'

'It is good when baby sleep, very long.' The big man laid his head on his joined hands, and laughed.

'Yes indeed it is. We're lucky that way.'

Kthunk! A billiard ball shot into a pocket.

'He like milk when he wake?'

'Oh yes. He'll have milk later.'

The big man went over to the bar and spoke confidentially to the barmaid. She left and came back with a glass of milk. The big man took the milk and gave it to the father.

'Thanks, but...'

'It is nothing. Niets.'

Martin, already tipsy, saw his chance. He got up from his chair and went over to the billiard table, put his hand on the big man's arm.

'Excuse me. It is not good for babies, this milk. You are very good to think of it, but his milk has to be special. Very *shhhpeshhal* milk for babies.'

The big man looked Martin up and down, and then down and up, and back up and down again, finally breaking into a smile.

'You very nice man. You will come home with me, yes?'

'I beg your pardon?' A voice spoke in clear English with a tone of menace.. 'Did you ask that floosie to come home with you, Adri?'

'What that to you, *stompzinnige?*' retorted the Big One.

An argument broke out between Martin's admirer and a fair-haired youth who had suddenly appeared from the other billiard table. The young man frequently turned aside from the spat to shower Martin with insults. The argument dragged on and blows were exchanged. Martin escaped through the door of the tavern, and stumbled up the lamplit street for a cab to take back to his lodgings.

As usual since he arrived in Sexbierum, Martin was out on Frau de Jong's veranda after breakfast the following day. He had brought out his laptop so that he could pretend to be typing excerpts from the weighty tome on the life of the Dutch admiral Tjerk Hiddes de Vries. But in reality he was thinking of the previous night, the Oude Geneva and the Big Billiard Player who had invited him back to his house.

He had wanted to be the Big Billiard Player's femme last night! He raised a hand to smooth his hair, a sign of frustration. *That bloody argument put paid to my chances. But maybe just as well.*

'Ah zo! There you are!'

The voice came from behind him just as a sizeable shadow fell over his table on the veranda. He recognised the voice. It was none other than that of the billiard player.

'My name is Adri. Adri de Root,' said Martin's visitor. 'I have come to apologise for the too quick way I was proposing to you last night. But I also wish to say that I am genuine in my enamourment of you. I was watching you, you were speaking with yourself at the lonely table. I saw you were a person of culture and delicacy, and I have not seen many of such in these barbaric days.'

Martin, all in a flutter, as casually as he could muster, invited Adri de Root to sit down. His eyes roved over the face opposite him, the broad forehead with one grey patch of hair in the middle of an otherwise bald head, the sagacious eyes with the kindly crows' feet, and was confirmed in his smittenness.

'It is I who should apologise to you,' he said. 'To be quite frank, and as you may have noticed, I had one Oude Genever too many. I was far too forward. But your English? It is much better than I thought.'

'Aha! Thank you! You noticed. I must explain that I am pretending to not have fluency because I am checking another player of billiards for a woman. She suspects he is being unfaithful. He is English, of course, and I play billiards with him because he loves this game and I hope he will meet some friends and reveal to them while I am listening. It is difficult. I lose every game of course.' Adri laughed indulgently. 'I am also sorry because of that silly jealous boy. But I have come to you because I wish to ask you to dinner with me. At my house. This evening.'

'Do you mean a date?'

'Well, to be quite frank, yes. I would like it to be a date. I would like if we have more than just dinner.'

'So you'd like me to be your Dolly Bird for the night?'

Adri laughed uproariously, and a series of barks erupted from the de Jongs' dog pound. 'Well, I would prefer to say that it could be a beginning,' he demurred. 'I will cook you an excellent dinner, and treat you to the contents of my cellar, and if everything goes well, after that we'll only be beginning.'

'Sounds good,' Martin said.

When Adri had departed, Martin went for his usual nap but

did not sleep for long, alert from anticipation.

Before leaving for his date, he knelt and said his prayers at the side of the bed. Instead of asking forgiveness for the whopping mortal sin he was about to commit, he asked God to bless his meeting with Adri that night, to let everything go well.

A big black hatchback, which had somewhat the appearance of a hearse, was waiting for him. The driver standing in the courtyard was a long bespectacled streak of misery who reminded Martin of Éamon deValera.

3

MARTIN'S GHOSTS

Martin woke up suddenly. A figure all in black was standing about ten feet away from him. A shiver down his spine told him that this was not a dream. The figure was there, for real, in the ample bedroom. The first thought that entered his mind was *It's the Angel of Death*.

Go réidh, a mhic. Be careful, son; in Irish, if you don't mind. He heard these words in his head, but the figure did not speak. It just stood there, large and strangely circular and black from head to foot, and solemn and terrifying, presaging death by its presence. Definitely graver than a piece of undigested gravy, because when Martin closed his eyes for a few seconds, the figure was still there when he re-opened them. He tried to pray, but he couldn't summon any conviction for the exercise: he was unable to inject any sincerity into the mantras of his God-bombardment.

After what seemed a very long time indeed, the figure disappeared, bringing with it Martin's sleep.

Sex and Death and the Other World had always been linked in Martin's mind. As the night wore sleeplessly on, he became convinced that he had been visited by some kind of spirit as a warning to stay away from sex, except of course marital sex which was allowed by Mother Church. In his experience, indulgence of his ecclesiastically disapproved sexual propensities had always seemed to call forth a response from beyond the grave. He especially remembered one night when, after a exceptionally torrid bout of auto-erotic fantasy, he was woken from sleep by the sight of an old crone, in an advanced state of putrefaction, leaning over his bed and cackling at him. The link between the masturbatory ritual and the cackling crone had seemed obvious to him: the one had called the other forth from a nearby grave.

As dawn began to tickle the curtains, however, his terror of the Angel of Death gave way to anger.

Frustration had happened at Adri's mansion. Smoke had begun to issue from a dish on the hob while they were snogging one another playfully, a fire alarm went off, nay, *two* alarms erupted ear-piercingly, putting the duo in a state of panic. Amid a lot of aimless to-ing and fro-ing, Adri eventually succeeded in phoning a company which, in turn, managed to neutralize one of the alarms, but the other alarm kept up its eardrum-splitting din for over an hour. The company disclaimed responsibility for the still-active alarm, suggesting that Adri must have had someone else install a second alarm system *to be sure to be sure,* belt as well as braces. It turned out that the second alarm could not be switched off remotely, the particular sensor which was causing the racket had to be located. The sensor was eventually found and the battery removed. But by this time, sex was the last thing on the couple's minds. Adri fed Martin a cold platter and drove him back to his pensione with little to say between them.

Why is it that every time I try to express my alter ego, something stupid like this happens? wondered Martin as he dressed for the new day.

Then he thought of the Angel of Death, and his anger gave way to returning fear. It was the *reality* of the figure that frightened him. People might try to explain away these things, but Martin felt he could distinguish between hallucinations and this kind of apparition, which resonated to the core of his being with the truth of its objective existence. Definitely not an undigested bit of beef. *Praise the Lord and pass the Apparition!* his Shadow, the Joker, quipped. The Apparition was duly awarded first class honours for Existence.

The question now remained, what did it *mean*?

'Why will you not even speak to me?' pleaded Adri.

'I told you,' Martin insisted, holding his patience, because this was the third time Adri had phoned that day. It was now five in the evening, and Martin had been woken from his afternoon nap. 'How often must I explain? Something very frightening happened me last night. I have come to regard it as a warning of impending death. And it seems to tie in very nicely with the whole damn fiasco of the smoke alarm.'

'What nonsense! Why don't you just admit that you have gone from me?'

'I haven't gone off you. I'm just afraid I'm going to die soon. And I want to be ready, if that's the case. '

'Why you not go out with a bang if you going to die? It is this stupid religion of yours.'

'Yes, Adri, it's this stupid religion of mine. Of course. The trouble is, I *believe* in it. Now will you let me have some peace of mind?'

'But maybe if Death has appeared to you, it does not mean that you is going to die. It could be somebody else.'

'Yes, I did think of that possibility, my friend. I have spent the day going over and over what the Apparition could possibly mean. The other strong contender for the meaning of this fright is that it is a warning. I mean, a warning that something bad will happen to me if I am unfaithful to my wife and indulge in sodomy.'

'Sodomy?' His would-be lover laughed sarcastically. 'It is so long since I hear that word.'

'Well that's as may be. Adri, you must know that I find you very attractive. If I could be convinced that the Apparition doesn't mean what I think it means, we could have a go at a bit of a liaison. Be patient.'

'I will wait, my friend, until hell freezes,' said the passionate suitor.

Martin had scarcely put his phone back in his pocket when it rang again. He pulled it back out and pleaded, 'Adri, will you give me a break!'

'Martin, it's Sarah. Are you all right?'

'Oh sorry Sarah, I thought you were someone else. This is a pleasant surprise.'

'Well, it's not really, Martin. I'm just ringing to say that the *gendarmerie* called here today. They wanted to talk to you about something. And who is this Adri?'

'Oh just a friend.'

'Drinking companion, no doubt.'

'We play billiards in the local. Over a pint or two. What did you say to the police?'

'I said you were in Holland. Have you any idea why they're looking for you?'

'Oh, probably a speeding fine or something.'

'I doubt it. They'd just send it to you in the post.'

'I have no idea. Mistaken identity, perhaps?'

'Anyway, I gave them your number. When are you coming home?'

'Sarah, dear, I'm barely left home.'

'I miss you.'

'I miss you too, love. But we discussed this. Things are going well so far. When I come home, I hope to be much better, less obsessive and impractical.'

'I'll drink to that, Martin.'

'Not too much, darling. See you soon. Love you.'

He put the phone down quickly, guiltily.

Martin is at his desk again today, trying to find some way of allowing himself a liaison with Adri. The Apparition has been going through the phases in his imagination. Fearsome and apocalyptic as it may have been, his memory now begins to detect in the grim features a slight trace of kindness, a sad tolerance of the infidelities that humanity gets up to and which will all be ironed out at the Second Coming, or even – who knows? – a good while before that.

'You must see the Fisherman's Village in Moddergat,' says the landlady, putting a bowl of soup and a crusty roll with Gouda before him. 'And the Wadden Zee. For a brek. You study very hard. Need refresh. Just, how you say, for Day Trek?'

'Day Trip,' smiled Martin, wishing she would leave him be at his veranda table.

'Ah yes, Day Trip, thank you. You will like.'

I most certainly will not like.

It was pleasant, after all, to go to Moddergat. His hired car had been lying in the pensione car park for over a week now, and the next day Martin decided he might as well put it to some use: who knows what possibilities of healing a change of scenery might bring? Besides, his landlady, Mrs What's-her-name, would be pleased if he followed her advice.

At Moddergat, there were steps leading up to the top of the dike beside the obelisk to drowned fishermen. He climbed them and viewed with shivery pleasure the hemline of mussel shells down below, on the seaward side, and beyond it a flatland of sand. He could hardly tell the sand apart from the sky, except in the foreground by the dark lines of breakwaters, and it was difficult to tell if there was, in fact, a sea. But there in the foreground of this Nothingscape, behold an astonishing field, with a few sheep and cattle! An impossible polderette, beyond the containment of the dike.

A windblown patch of sunlight dragged its anchor, and above the flap of wind, he could hear a seabird piping, night-noises of a child. The dike's flank, on its seaward side, was a tarred velodrome, a gull's graveyard

'Moeilijk' said a voice behind him. He turned and saw a rotund, bespectacled man who began to gesticulate and babble at him in a friendly fashion. Throughout his fulsome discourse – was it Dutch or Friesian? – that same word resounded like a passing bell, until its speaker became transfigured into a bell tower in the bemused sightseer's mind. The man finally flapped his hands in mock despair, laughed heartily and descended the steps.

Martin guessed the eccentric man was talking about the economic impossibility of this place. And his thoughts led him naturally to the contrast whereby the most economically unpromising places are also the most aesthetically evocative. 'You can't eat the scenery' as they'd say in Ireland.

By this time, the day had changed: the sun had asserted itself against the Nothingscape, and Martin decided it mightn't be any harm to take a little walk.

The dike stretched away in a huge sweeping curve. The sea was to the right of him glimmering in the sun, a silvery grey, and to the left was the rich tillage of a polder, dark green acres of potatoes, tracts of ripening wheat, the red pyramids of farmhouses. People began to appear in twos and threes, spreading rugs on the now-grassy seaward side. The path ahead of him became a mirage of bright water flames, burning, evaporating. He began to perspire.

After about half-an-hour, he was relieved to see a café on the seaward side of the dike, with slipways running down to the sea. The cafe had a veranda rather like the one at Frau de Yong's. Martin immediately occupied one of the tables and ordered a coffee.

'Can you tell me,' he asked the waitress when she brought him his coffee, 'there is a word – it sounds like 'moylik' – can you tell me what it means?'

'Ah *Moeilijk*!' exclaimed the waitress. 'But this in English I do not know.'

'Difficult,' said a man sitting two tables away from him. 'Not easy.'

Like my life, thought Martin. 'Thanks.'

Leaving his religious order, Martin had been shell-shocked when he arrived in London. His spiritual director had advised him to go to the UK: at that time in Ireland, they still had hang-ups about 'failed priests'.

'Martin, they'll eat you out there!' the director had thundered, to frighten him off his resolve to leave. And how right he was:

Martin had dream-walked his way through London in PTSD for years, achieving nothing. If he managed to ask a young woman on a date, he felt obliged to tell her the whole story of his religious crisis and end by saying 'But I'm all right now' in an unconvincing manner which convinced the young woman that he was far from all right. He was damaged goods, haunted, struggling even with his teaching job in a Catholic School in Finchley, unable to handle a relatively civilized lot of giddy adolescent boys. He clammed up if a woman began to talk to him at a party. He was rich in sensitivity and nothing else.

Everything seemed strange in the big wide world. He was a bit like the Poor Clare nun dropped by taxi at a busy train station who asked a passer-by 'Has there been an accident?'

One morning at breakfast, a fellow boarder in his first lodgings in London was singing the praises of André Previn. Martin had seen the celebrity on television, and opined that he thought the man was pretentious, for which remark he received the response 'Haven't you heard, Fuckface? André Previn is one of the greatest conductors in the world.'

Fuckface. That was the kind of countenance he carried around with him. Everything was too strange and moving too fast. And too fake and pretentious. And his face was hollowed out by guilt.

But before he left his monastery, there was one easy-going priest who said something to him that turned out to be prophetic: that he would find a woman who would put up with him and his damaged self. She would listen to his story sympathetically, not as if she fully understood it, but accepted him and his wooly-minded mystical aftershock. And that woman had been Sarah, who actually liked what she called his 'wooly thoughts'. How could that priest have been so sure he would meet someone like Sarah?

But would his wife accept his sexual fluidity? Would she not consider his gallivanting with Adri as betrayal? Of course she would! Somehow he knew, in the midst of all his fantasy, that his present course would be a bridge too far for Sarah.

He was thinking these thoughts and sipping his coffee, when the man who had translated *moeilijk* caught his eye. 'Do you mind if I join you for a little while?' And before Martin could answer, the translator was seated at his table, facing him.

'Excuse me for being so forward, but I can see that you are in very big trouble,' said the soft-spoken, slender, sad-faced man who had just seated himself in front of Martin.

He could not credit what he was hearing. There was a *clunk!* as he dropped his cup, spilling a splash of coffee and chipping the saucer.

'I beg your pardon. What did you just say?'

'I am really very sorry to be the bearer of bad tidings. But I see, from studying your face, your posture, your eye-movements, and chiefly from your aura which I am picking up, that you are in very great trouble. Very great danger indeed.'

'I have never seen you before in my life, and you have the effrontery to tell me this. Who the hell are you, anyway?'

'It is not important who I am. What's important is my gift of vision. My poor man, my heart goes out to you. Nevertheless, what I have said I cannot retract.'

'Excuse me. I am not in the humour at the moment for male Cassandras. Would you mind terribly if I asked you to fuck off?'

Martin attempted to rise, but found he could not stir, held on his seat by the power of the intruder's eyes. *He holds him with his glittering eye.*

'My friend, you are in the grip of what, in theological terms, we call an *Obsession*.'

Martin vaguely remembered a theology lesson in his seminary where the meanings of obsession and possession were defined and distinguished, but he had forgotten the gist of the lesson. He was, however, quickly filled in by his unwelcome companion.

'Obsession, from the Latin *obsidere* – to besiege – is a form of insanity caused by the persistent attack of a besieging spirit from *outside* the individual. Obsession is the opposite of Possession, which is control by an invading spirit *from within*. Both, however, involve the usurpation of the person's individuality, identity, and the taking control of body and mind by an evil incorporeal entity.'

'Come again?'

'Specifically, in your case, you are being obsessed by a spirit – maybe more than one – which attacks the sexual dimension. You are particularly vulnerable to such an attack because you have experienced religious ecstasy. In the words of T. S. Eliot, your spirit is 'unappeased and peregrine'. It seeks something to fill the gaping void left in you by the absence of God's visitations to your soul. You seek compensation in greater and greater carnal gratification with its temporary sense of fulfilment. Meanwhile your attacker, either in the form of a succubus, incubus or by supplying your imagination with potent sexual images and energies, seeks to extend and fluff out your range of sexual proclivities. You have begun to stray from stable partnership, with its salutary give-and-take, towards the shape-shiftings of auto-eroticism. You will look for partners who flatter your increasingly shifting sexual vanity until, by the time this wicked work is finished, you will be exhausted and fit only for confinement to a psychiatric institution.'

There was silence at the table, during which the sound of the hissing espresso machine could be heard from within the café. At last, Martin spoke.

'Do you know who you remind me of? The priests and teachers of my childhood who used to frighten us with tales of diabolical possession and tell us that the Devil puts all kinds of bad ideas into a child's head. *Bless me Father for I have sinned, but the Devil made me do it.* The lingo you are using merely puts a gloss of learning on all that mumbo jumbo.'

'The Devil's greatest trick, my friend, is to convince people that he doesn't exist.'

'Quite the opposite: we are kept in thrall to these superstitions and fears by circular arguments like the one you've just used.'

'And yet you still keep up the regular practice of prayer, I believe? You pray to be delivered from evil ghosts?'

Martin groped for a response.

The soft-spoken one rose gently. 'I must go. You have been snarled in the thorny branches of debauchery, my son, because you have abandoned God's calling and chosen the fleshpots of Egypt. You are a half-baked angel, my child. Sexual confusion will attend you all your life. My heart goes out to you. Very soon you will be provided with proof of my honest credentials. '

'I doubt it very much. Oh, and thanks a million for ruining my day.'

Martin turned away from his mealy-mouthed Counsellor From Nowhere, fearful that he might clock him one and equally fearful that his fist might fly through an incorporeal face. He went to pay for his coffee – and apologize stammeringly for the chipped saucer.

As Martin left the café, the barista eyed the waitress, placing the tip of his pointing index finger on his forehead, twisting his wrist to suggest a screwdriver loosening a screw.

Martin headed back the way he came, mocked in his distress by the *mbaaas* of sheep.

4

HENRY AND OSCAR

There was a man having breakfast in the courtyard of a hotel in L'Escarene, just above Nice, in the Pays Nicoise. His car was parked on a steep incline within the grounds, under a huge viaduct, with two stones wedged against the front wheels in case of slippage. The sun glinted on a small swimming pool, and he was reading, as best he could, an article in *Le Monde* about the tenth anniversary of the Good Friday Agreement.

Earlier, before eight, he had taken a walk through nearby streets which were already brimming. He marvelled at a group of women, chatting animatedly as they rinsed clothes in an ornately carved Ancient Roman tub of stone. He was fascinated both by the communality of the event and the use of such a precious relic of the past for a menial everyday task.

He had left Holland because the Dutch police had called looking for him at his guest house and his landlady could not endure the thought of a guest who was being sought by the police. What would the neighbours think?

In vain, he protested his innocence, said his goodbyes to a tearful admirer, and decided to head for Umbria, where an old friend was running an agritourist establishment.

He drove to Paris, refused to allow his conscience's appeals that he should drop in to see his wife, extended his car rental at the airport and drove to the L'Escarene hotel. He had been there once before, years ago.

Laying *Le Monde* aside, he began to ponder the kinks in time where the eternal breaks in on the temporal. He had experienced one in Croatia a few years before, waking from a siesta: a line of angels were standing on a highway of golden clouds with their backs to him, and seemed to be trembling (with joy?) at what they beheld further up the road. Croatia, of course, had a very famous kink at Medugorje, where the Virgin had appeared to herald and warn of the terrible civil war. And he had personally experienced at least two kinks in Friesland: the Apparition and the Prophet of Doom. And what of the dog who humped him? It was a mercy that he was heading for Italy.

It would take him most of the day to get to his friend's place in Umbria. The morning, in early September, was already hotting up; he would need to be heading off soon.

'What in the name of God am I doing?' the traveller kept asking himself as he drove past the Hundred Tunnels around Genova, skirting Florence and Arezzo, leaving the Autostrada at Bettolle, following signs for Perugia and Magione on the dual carriageway. 'Why am I behaving like Orestes fleeing from the Eumenides?'

He spent his journey going over various possible actions of his which might have attracted police attention.

*He had killed someone while night-driving, a bump which he thought was a fox or a badger had turned out to be a person. The incident had been caught on Dashcam footage.

*A boy in his school had reported him for sexual abuse.

*He had downloaded child porn to his laptop.

*He had raped someone, killed someone, raped and killed someone.

*He had embezzled serious funds from one of the school's accounts.

*He was involved with drug dealing.

'Surely,' he thought, 'if I had done any of those things, I would have remembered.' But the traveller and his memory had an unusual relationship: he knew that it was best to flee, he was sure he had done *something* which merited the interest of the police, but he didn't know what he had done or how bad, or even terrible, it was. Whatever it was he had perpetrated, it was not available to consciousness. But a very ominous aura clung to the absence, which pooh-poohed the possibility that he had been framed or that he was innocent. It must have happened a few years ago, he speculated, and the police have only just caught up with me.

He got on to the single carriageway outside Magione, followed the GPS directions and turned right before the ascent to Castel Rigone, at a sign marked *Podere*, bumping along a dusty boreen flanked by flat acres of maize and hilly olive groves. He arrived at the gravelly forecourt of the farmhouse, got out to be greeted by a dog barking suspiciously, and a kerchief-headed woman calling *Benvenuto in Umbria!*

'Ah, welcome indeed,' said the portly Irish proprietor, who emerged from the farmhouse after the charlady.

The new arrival's name is Martin but he now calls himself Henry. He explains the change of name convolutedly to his friend Oscar, the proprietor of the agritourist farm, as being due to the fact that he had been christened Henry Martin Kelly, but his parents always called him Martin, because his father was called Harry, but he himself, Martin, would prefer to be called Henry (but certainly not Harry), if Oscar didn't mind.

In a privet tree's shade, which took the edge off the still-strong heat of the September afternoon, they sat drinking wine on old chairs, Italian but reminiscent of Irish sugawn, on a patio at the back of the farmhouse. Behind them was a bluff, falling to the flat valley bottom, where revolving sprinklers cascaded veils of water over maize and fruit trees.

'So you are Henry II, but prefer to be called plain Henry?' joked Oscar. 'Anyway, Henry II was a right bastard, wasn't he, because he got the Normans to invade Ireland.'

'My father, Harry I, was also a bit of a bastard,' said Henry.'

'At least you haven't suppressed his bastardhood.'

Henry winced uneasily at the mention of suppression. 'No, I have very clear memories of him beating the crap out of me.

On the other hand, there may be something else that I have completely suppressed...'

'And what is that, my child?' asked Oscar in a mock tone of the Confessional.

'But it's suppressed, Oscar. I don't know what it is. Or even *if* it is. A therapist once told me I was suffering from stress and perhaps I am prone to imagining things. Anyway, coming here has taken the edge off my *angst*. I definitely needed to return, for the nostalgia and the peace. I'm only here a week, and I already feel like a new man.'

'So it's Goodbye Martin, Hello Henry,' quipped the portly proprietor of *Agritourismo Paradiso*. 'But as far as I can see, you haven't changed a bit. And I mean that in a good way. You're easy to live with, as always.'

Henry was close to tears. 'Thanks, Oscar. This is a real haven for me.'

'Stay as long as you like.'

Several weeks of bliss followed for Henry. He spent euphoric mornings sipping coffee on the back patio under the privet tree, dreamily undemanding afternoons at a bathing and sunbathing haunt on the shores of Lake Trasimene. He dined with his cordial host or at Pub Franci in the town of Magione. Oscar had an old three-wheeled Vespa which he tuned up for his now carless guest, and Henry drove it to the lake and once ventured into Perugia on it, to view the National Gallery of Umbria and the Fountain. But he did not go into the city's churches, though he admired the pink marble of their facades.

He phoned Sarah dutifully twice a week to tell her of his progress and to reassure her about his improved mental health. He lived a chaste life, said his prayers and was not visited by incubi, succubi or apparitions. He resumed contact with Facebook Friends and texted them with bits of innocuous news and photographs he had taken. Everything was going well, and there were no calls from the police.

And then a minor disturbance happened. One day a message

appeared on his Facebook feed from a previously unknown account, as follows:

Hi, I understand that texting in your private space is inconvenient, and I apologize for that, but I find you very attractive and classy. It would be foolish and cowardly of me to skip over your profile without saying hello. Since I have some free time, I've decided to bring to your attention how lovely you are and how wonderful it would be if we could become friends.

The sender was purportedly a much-decorated, retired American Army General who lived in Iraq.

After much hesitation and soul searching over the rest of the day, Henry's vanity prevailed and he decided to reply to the message: *Hi, thank you for your kind words. DM me on Messenger.*

Not long passed before his Messenger peeped a reply: *Hi, just a little about myself. Do I prefer big or small breasts? Answer: Neither, I prefer no breasts but I like erect nipples. I am also an expert on finding the Agnate G-Spot. May I send you my Prospectus? Yours truly, Generalissimo Spanky-Poohs. PS I no longer live in Iraq. I have moved to Italy and live very close to you.*

Despite the revelation that his correspondent was close by, Henry was crestfallen at the mention of a catalogue. He wasn't deluded and self-absorbed enough not to cop that this personage or business was probably offering sex for money. At the same time, the first message had re-awakened his erotic urges, and he wanted to see where this correspondence would lead. He was suddenly full of longing to be held and fondled, to be kissed and caressed, to be loved and made love to. He messaged back:

You may send me your catalogue. The response was immediate: *Attached please find Prospectus. I so look forward to meeting you. xxx*

PROSPECTUS OF INTERVENTIONS
(1) Anal Intercourse Puro €250
(2) Anal Intercourse With Foreplay and Finding of Agnate G-Spot €500
(3) Fellation Puro €250

(4) Fellation With Foreplay, and Spanking by Third Party €500
(5) Spanking Bondage, Leading to Orgasm €500
(6) Spanking Bondage With Disparagement, Leading to Orgasm €700
(1) and (3) €700
(2) and (4) €1,000
Complete Package €2,000
Complete Package with Dinner and Taxi €2,500
Confession Post Factum from Resident Priest €1,000
Please complete Form on Website to order Interventions. All major credit cards accepted.

Henry's first thought was, No problem, I have the money. His second thought was, Wow, that's brilliant, they've thrown in a priest as well! His third thought was, Note the *xxx*. His fourth thought was, I am going to take this, I know I am going to take it, all €3,500 worth, may the Lord forgive me. But I'll hold for a while, in case they think I'm a complete sucker.

He sent a note on Messenger: *Prospectus received with thanks. Will study.* A ding responded immediately, *Happy perusal!*.

Dithering around for the rest of the day, he visited Oscar's library, a very elegant room with carved wooden panelling and shelves upon shelves of disorganized books belying its ornate features. He plucked out a random book and found that it was Vaclav Havel's *Letters to Olga*. He tried to read the Preface, but couldn't concentrate.

He went to his room, had a pre-dinner nap, and woke up still dithering mentally. As he was groping his way up the dimly lit stone stairs to Oscar's apartment, he heard a voice singing merrily from the balcony:

Gigolo, gigolo, I am just a Gigolo
I will do your bidding underneath the mistletoe
Gigolo, gigolo, I am just a gigolo
I will do your bidding, long goodbye or quick hello

Gigolo, gigolo, I am just a gigolo
You will do my bidding, I will play your piccolo

He looked up and saw the wide back of Oscar, the head thrown back in ditty-rendition, as he laid knives and forks on the balcony table. Suddenly distressed, Henry retraced his steps down the stairs. The awful thought had occurred to him that the retired American general was none other than his landlord.

He sat on the armchair in his apartment for another ten minutes, berating himself for thinking that the singing of a silly ditty about a gigolo could possibly implicate Oscar in the operation of an expensive online male-oriented brothel. Then he gathered his courage to face the badly-lit stone steps again, and Oscar Take Two.

On the landlord's balcony in late September, it was still balmy at dusk. After a dinner of grilled radicchio with olive oil and parmesan, followed by roast chicken and potatoes, and panna cotta for dessert, Oscar and Henry were silently savouring a digestif of Nocino. The resident peacock had taken up a perch in an oak tree on the edge of the bluff, and occasionally uttered a scream of enraged dignity. Out of the blue, Oscar declaimed:

'Awakened within a dream,
I fall into my own arms.
....What kept you so long?'

After a pause like a printer's when given the command to print, Henry said 'Interesting. I often want to fall into my own arms.'
'Really?'
'Some would call it auto-eroticism,' ventured Henry. It was his second aperitif and the Nocino was very strong. 'I suppose they'd say I fancy myself. Or, as the cruder ones would put it, that I'd like to get up on myself.'
'So if you fall in love with someone, it is simply a case that they confirm your self-love? That they are the substitute for the

impossible act of getting up on yourself?'

'They are the confirmation to me of the beauty, the *allure*, which I see in myself,' Henry proclaimed. And then, poutily, after a pause, 'And which you obviously *don't* see in me.'

'I can see your allure, yes, but I have had affairs with some who were just as you describe yourself, and the relationships simply fizzled out. All the temper tantrums. No give and take, you see. All one-way traffic. On both sides, I have to confess.'

'It seems to be how fate has hard-wired me, and yet prevented me from being what I really am,' Martin sighed loudly, bitterly, almost in tears.

'There, there, have some more Nocino,' said Oscar, rising to fill his glass. 'But that haiku I just quoted – you surely don't think it has anything to do with auto-eroticism?'

'Doesn't it? Sounded like that to me.'

'It would be like saying St John of the Cross was writing his mystical poetry about a stunner he chanced on when taking a stroll outside his monastery. But the poem has to do with falling into the arms of everything really, of being one with the universe.'

'Which I most certainly am not,' said Martin with a tone of petulance which was echoed in a squawk from the peacock.

Henry told Oscar about the Facebook messages he had received from Generalissimo Spanky-poohs.

'I was doing fine, marvellously in fact, I didn't know myself, and then this incursion re-awakened my sexual hunger again.'

Oscar was silent for a while, then he said: 'Maybe you need a good ride, maybe you don't. Maybe I can help you, maybe I can't. We'll see.'

By now it was dark. 'Let me guide you down the stairs,' said Oscar, holding his groggy friend by the arm.

I was SO humiliated. I mean to say, God! – THESE PEOPLE! the peacock squawked.

Glimpsed and lost sight of by turns as it rounded many bends, a car was heading towards the farm along the white road, kicking up the late September dust.

They were sitting on the patio having lunch, Henry and Oscar, and Henry was trying to tell Oscar about his foiled attempts to score with Adri. He wasn't doing very well, partly because he could see that Oscar wasn't all that interested, but mainly because he felt a pinprick sensation of the uncanny as he watched and listened to the car's approach.

There was never much traffic on the *strada bianca*, but still.... it wasn't the fact of a car that aroused his eerie sensation; since he arrived, there had been no other car that spooked him.

The car drove past the farm, and Henry thought he could see a woman with dark glasses peer from the driver's window. Shortly the same car came back, giving Henry another pinprick sensation. The pinprick seem to be telling him the car was from the future. Impossible! He looked away.

'I hope you don't mind, but sex talk makes me uneasy,' Oscar said as he rose to fetch the dessert. 'I suppose it has to do with being sexually abused in boarding school as a child.'

How many were abused in Irish boarding schools, all told? wondered Henry. *It must have been a Pandemic.*

No matter what I do, Henry typed on his laptop later on, *and it's all very wonderful and all that, to be able to do so many kinds of things, but no matter what I do, I'm not satisfied. So there! The only thing that would satisfy me is forbidden by my conscience, and that is to have TOTALFUCK. That is why I have booked a quasi-religious orgy from Generalissimo Spanky-poohs, complete with an audience, and with me as the oblation to be sexily offered up. This will not only be a source of intense pleasure to myself, but also a revenge on the Church for the damage it has inflicted on me.*

May the Lord forgive me and welcome me back to his good books after the event, but I am determined to see it through. The priest I have paid for will of course absolve me, but I'm skeptical of such a sordid use of the Confessional.

Martin read what he had written and deleted it immediately. Later on, lying in bed, he remembered his former primary teacher in Ireland. The man had been to Japan for a spell and brought back with him one of Basho's famous haikus, which he often quoted in the rural classroom without translation.

What was it again? It was so beautiful. Martin used to quote it in Japanese to his students at the lycée. His primary teacher had explained that the haiku was about the wind in the reeds sounding like human voices, and added that the last line could also mean the act of mouth-to-mouth feeding.

How did the haiku go?... Ah yes!

obi no koe
koya akikaze no
kuchi utsushi

(Voices in the reeds
this is the mouth mimicry
of the autumn wind)

Martin was glad he hadn't forgotten those Japanese words and said the haiku to himself over and over. It was sad, he thought, that his teaching job conspired to exhaust him with its analytic approach to the Literature Syllabus, so that he didn't have time for poetry any more, it bored him to death to be dissecting poems. But he never forgot that haiku, and the feeling he had when he spoke it to himself, the sense that it told of a world before disaster, or perhaps of a parallel universe. The words were like a spell that brought him back to the Origin, the connectedness of everything.

An Irish poet friend who also lived in Paris once told him that a woman came up to him after a reading and said, 'I loved your poem about snow'. The poet had never alluded to snow during the reading, but nevertheless granted that the woman's response was valid. If something in the poem led her back to the world-before-disaster, her childhood perhaps, to a state of original wonder, that was good, and very good.

Basho's famous crow, from another haiku Martin had learned

by heart, was perhaps the dreaded Figure in Black or one of its avatars, and he resolved that if the figure ever appeared to him again, he would recite it. He now felt that the apparition was the fearsome custodian of the innocent realm, permitting no one to enter except the pure, whom the purity of poetry helped return to their origins.

The haiku had a mysterious reality about it, an opaque solidity. It was a talisman which could break the hold of the Figure in Black.

He cancelled his booking with Generalissimo Spanky-poohs, accepting the loss of his fifty per cent deposit for default, all because of the feelings the memory of these haikus invoked in him.

But boredom continued to spread its domain in his spirit. The weather was getting colder, the Tramontana wind struck earlier in October than usual, and his beach resort was summarily shut down for the winter. Oscar seemed to go into his shell with the coming of the spell of wind from the Alps, the warning that Winter was not far away. And apart from Oscar, Martin knew no one. He needed some kind of excitement. He decided to visit Rome.

5

CHRISTY

Christopher Christ-Bearer, uncertain as to identity or even existence, big and strong, carried the Infant Jesus across the flooded river. That's the name which a young Irish emigrant to England has adopted for himself in his private reveries. Reduced to Christy in the real world, he is anyone, no one, somewhere between no one and anyone, or between anyone and some one, but definitely not Somebody. Engaged in a futile search for his own importance, a tin whistle player, God help us, who has been asked to toot his flute at the BBC in Shepherd's Bush for an in-house training programme. He thought it was going to be a real programme, his big chance, but it won't go public, not even on Channel 1,999. It's a piece for the training archives.

He gives tin whistle lessons on Tuesday evenings in an upstairs room in a pub on Fulham Broadway. The pub is called 'The White Hart' and it's run by a cousin of his, so he gets the room free. Luckily, seeing that he's officially unemployed, and it's a source of extra income to add to the dole.

I should have let that Hilary lad go on kissing me, he thinks, looking back at what happened in Shepherd's Bush, *and then suggest that he takes lessons. I'm sure he would have jumped at the idea, seeing that he obviously had the hots for me, and especially when he learned that the tuition is one on one. I'm not so sure I'd have been able to keep his advances at bay, but I wouldn't have sneezed at the chance of earning another tenner a week.*

Christy lives in a squat which has not yet been cleared by bailiffs. He has a room to himself and a double-bed mattress with a psychedelic quilt, and some old overcoats hanging in the wardrobe for winter. That is, if he's not thrown out before the cold weather arrives. He also has a broken electric fire, which he found in a skip, and it'll be grand if he can get a new element for it. He cooks for himself on a little Campingaz stove.

When Christy first came to the UK, he spent a few weeks working on a building site in Stevenage. A friend of a friend from home in Ireland was a ganger on the site and got him the job. It was easy work, because the construction was winding down. Sweeping floors and smoothing lumps off concrete walls with a Kango. Spending long breaks smoking and talking to a workmate from Belfast who would shout at him: 'For fucks sake, hey! Would ya lay that down and come over for a chat.'

Or so it was, a bit of a doddle, until Christophoros Christ-Bearer was betrayed by thirty pieces of timber. Imagine being left on one's own to figure out how to bring thirty long narrow beams of timber to the thirteenth floor of a new post office exchange building? That nearly led to disaster, because Christy figured the crane could lift the timber and run it in to the scaffolding of the thirteenth floor. But there was some kind of outcrop on the fourteenth floor that prevented the crane from carrying the timber in far enough to land and unload. It stopped within an arm's stretch, swaying gently back and forth, in abeyance. But when he attempted to pull it in further by grabbing one of its chains, he had the appalling sensation of being hoisted into open space on the outswing of the load. Just in time, he managed to grab a railing of the scaffolding with his other hand and lift himself back on to the platform, while the individual beams of timber began to slip from their chains, and plummet to the ground. Luckily there was no one passing by down below at the time.

One by one, Martin had to start carrying the beams up the stairs, which involved a day's work and having to put up with quips from other workers as he headed up his hill of Golgotha, a beam on his shoulder.

As soon as he had enough tin whistle students to scrimp an existence, Christy gave up being a builder's labourer. Although the wages were a lot better than the income from tutoring, he no longer had to get up and be in Cricklewood at half-six in the morning for the van, and wrestle in the back with the spare tyre and tools for a bit of comfort.

Conscious of having been spared death or serious mutilation, he would occasionally waive the tuition fee offered by some poor student who looked a bit the worse for wear – as if the few pieces of timber life threw the lad's way were beginning to shape into a serious cross.

He has this persistent idea that his full name, Christopher – Christophoros, the Christ-bearer – actually implicates him in a destiny. This is an obsessional thought rather than a conviction, a cause of fantasies rather than action. He's all action in the fantasies, founding cooperatives among the unemployed, bringing the poor across the rough waters that separate the social classes. He's not even really sure if he believes in Christ, but his thoughts and fantasies are very intrusive. He now has a lot of time on his hands: time to indulge long bouts of day-dreaming, with him as the hero, the Christ-carrier, and even more time left over to ponder why he's doing it. He's never told any of his friends about it, not even Paddy. He keeps his mask on, the Irish emigrant's mask of the hard man.

The only way this Christ-bearer obsession has seeped into reality is through his tin whistle lessons. He can see the joy he's bringing to some of his pupils as they begin to get the hang of a tune, its rhythm and phrasing, after working on it for weeks. There is a wide river to be crossed between knowing the notes of a reel and playing them so that they actually sound like a reel.

A pupil comes in beaming from ear to ear, sits down and plays a tune he's been learning and Christy asks him 'What's the difference between what you played just now and what you played last week?' The student replies 'It sounds like a reel now' and Christy says 'You've cracked it, well done'. And that's when he gets the feeling of being a Christ-carrier, the sense that he has brought a person across rough waters to a happier place.

He went along to Shepherd's Bush with Paddy, his Republican friend who plays the bodhrán, and there he met Hilary the gay tin whistle player who had only begun to learn the whistle but knew the trainee producer from meeting him on the plane from Rome to London. Christy thought Hilary was so shapely he could pass for a girl, a real stunner minus the breasts.

And to tell the truth, he was within a whisker of being seduced, just about preserving his macho image. When the recording session was over and they were waiting for the trainee producer to bring the pitiful contract for signing, he carried Hilary across the waters of a tune called 'The Dogs among the Bushes' – there in Shepherd's Bush, where they were dogs among the Shepherd's Bushites. Hilary kissed him and as sure as God, he felt an erection coming on. There was a waft of perfume, and the androgyne beauty, putting his hands on the lapels of Christy's jacket, leaned into him for longer than a thank-you would permit....

'I swear I wanted to do it, right there in the back room of the studio,' Christy confessed to another mate, a poet friend he boozed with in 'The Pineapple' in Kentish Town. 'Oh Jesus when I think of him, all my notions about life fly out the window and I ask myself *What the fuck is this thing beauty?* He continued to push his lips onto mine, and when I looked over at Paddy, didn't he give me a wink the same as if a girl was kissing me.'

But Christy was feeling pretty rancorous about having to bestir himself to go to what turned out to be his great non-appearance on BBC TV. He disengaged himself abruptly from the upsettingly persistent embrace, said his goodbyes and left. Paddy told him later that the shocked disappointment on Hilary's face was a sight to behold. It was as if he'd never been rebuffed by anyone before, and couldn't understand it. Paddy felt sorry for him, invited him for a pint at The Shepherd and Flock. In fact, he shacked up with Hilary for a couple of days, being the kind of bloke who doesn't particularly care what gender the eye-candy is as long as it's eye-candy.

Hilary invited him to stay in his plush apartment in Islington and when Paddy asked him how he could afford such luxury, he was met with a finger to the lips. But it turned out that Hilary was a real drama queen and when he left London for a trip back to Rome, Paddy took the opportunity to leave the flat.

'It was the periods in between that I couldn't stand,' he told Christy, 'having to listen to him going on and on about himself and his *allure*, as he called it. About being a rent boy in Rome and how he was trying to get away from it. About how his beauty was landing him in all kinds of tight situations. About all the politicians and celebrities that fell for him at first sight. Pestering me about how beautiful I thought he was. And so on for all eternity.'

A few weeks later Paddy mentioned Hilary again, on a sunny day in October when the two friends were walking back from Hampstead Heath to a bus stop, dragging their hurleys along behind them after pucking a *sliotar* around in Parliament Hill Fields.

Paddy plays hurling because it's an Irish thing to do, Christy tags along for the exercise. Neither of them are much good, and they'd never make it, even on to the subs' bench of one of the London hurling teams, which are below par compared to the teams back in Ireland.

'Hilary was a rent boy in Rome, a sort of upmarket one,' Paddy said, taking a swipe with his stick at a dandelion on the edge of the path. 'He told me how he had a client – his keeper, as he called him – who sets him up in hotels or apartments whenever he takes the notion to visit a place. And that's why he was ensconced in luxury in Islington, the little faggot.'

They stood at a bus-stop beside Parliament Hill Fields with the hurleys on their shoulders like upside-down rifles. They could have been on the side of a country road at home, waiting to be picked up by their team's minibus.

'He has a whole fucking ideology about his own beauty,' Paddy went on. 'That's the shite I couldn't put up with. I wouldn't have minded the biographical stuff. But I've been thinking about that other palaver for the last few weeks. It kept coming back to me. And now I find it very disturbing, Christy. Very disturbing.'

'Maybe you still have the hots for him.'

'Ah for fuck's sake, Christy!'

Paddy went into a sulk, and Christy regretted his remark. He had been getting uncomfortable, which was usual whenever his friend went into deep mode. They were skirting the zone where what disturbed Paddy didn't disturb him. It was one of those occasions when a person would want his bus to come quickly. But of course it didn't, and neither did Paddy's. They were in the mid-afternoon bus-doldrums.

'I'm sorry, Paddy. I was being a bit flippant.'

'OK.' Paddy turned away, still sore.

'If the truth must be known,' Christy further conceded, 'I got a bit of a horn myself when he tried to kiss me.'

Paddy was appeased by the confession. 'I thought you did, all right,' he laughed.

'What is this physical beauty all about?'

It was meant as a harmless rhetorical question, but Paddy furrowed his brows fiercely and, after a long pause, he replied: 'By God, 'tis a hard pancake, that one. A tough chestnut, all right.'

After another long pause, he went on: 'Do you know, I think he has you in his sights? A friend of mine told me his current method is to dress up as a woman and score with some half-ossified fella? And he does unexpected calls, if he gets to know an address of someone he fancies. You'd want to watch out for a late night visit.'

'You're havin' me on,' Christy grinned, and there was his bus, pulling in.

On the way back to his squat, he was preoccupied with Hilary, feeling a little sorry for him, remembering his needy kiss at the BBC. But he wouldn't have liked to be deceived by a man dressed up as a woman. That would have really put him off.

Hilary didn't come to him like that. A few weeks later he came naked, straight into his bed. But Christy was having none of it, although he allowed the intruder to sleep with him for the night.

5

MARTIN'S ROME JOURNAL

Sunday 01 November

Here I am in the Eternal City after several weeks' delay. The hold-up was because Oscar insisted that I couldn't go to Rome without sorting out my Residency Permit. 'In case you get into trouble,' he said. I was rather miffed by his insistence on my having a stupid Residency Permit. Of course, it means I must get back to being Martin again while in Rome, as that is the only forename on my passport.

I am staying in a well-appointed hostel run by the Catholic Church (who else?) near the Colosseum. It's quite rainy here, although the weather is still mild.

On my first day I was surrounded by a pregnant pickpocket and her accomplices at Termini, and on the second I was inveigled to sit in his car by a con man who pretended to recognize me. Oscar had warned me about Termini and I beat an instant retreat from the pickpocket and her entourage, but I wasn't as quick to twig the con man.

He was in his early fifties, generously grey-bearded and grey-haired without being too exuberantly hirsute: the look of an ageing, reined-in hippie. Crow's feet led into eyes which held a faint gleam of that first fine careless rapture. He was a deadbeat, an urban desperado. He knew me from the early nineties, he said. We had been friends in London. Saying he now worked in fashion, he showed me a photograph, without a logo, of a male model wearing a suit. He wanted to give me a jacket in memory of our friendship. Pulling a sickly looking mustard-coloured one, wrapped in cellophane, from the back seat of the car, he planted it on my lap. It is free, he said. For you, my friend. The only problem was he needed a little money for petrol....

At last I understood. I moved quickly, slamming the car door behind me, lugging my two Despar shopping bags up the hill to my digs, hoping he wouldn't follow me. He didn't.

The guests here in the Borgo Irlandese are predominantly Irish, coming to celebrate their own or a relative's Roman Wedding, to visit their sons in the seminary next door or for a bit of sightseeing. But the place has become more generally renowned as a hospitable and relatively cheap B&B, and more and more Italians and other nationals are using it. The Colosseum, that most iconic of Roman sights, is only fifteen minutes' walk away and although the district is unprepossessing, it is quiet and fairly central.

Monday 02 November

The two incidents that occurred during my first two days took the shine off my enthusiasm somewhat, made me wary and feeling lonely. I decided to try and contact the only two people I knew who lived in Rome, Claudia and Claudio, who were originally from Umbria. Luckily they still had the same phone number from years ago and were living in the same small apartment with the man's mother and their son. I presumed they were still relatively hard up (otherwise they would surely have moved house) so I decided to invite them to dinner at a restaurant called The Golden Ass. Coincidentally, it was in an area common both to me and my friends, and was the only restaurant in the area that The Michelin Guide had given a star. I phoned and booked a table for Friday evening.

I set off to check out the restaurant. Walking from my lodgings at the Borgo in the direction of the Colosseum, I noticed a group of nuns outside the Chiesa di Santi Quattro, gathered round a small Peugeot car in the forecourt of the church. One was hoovering through the front passenger door, two were wiping the outside surface with wet sponges, and one was foot-pumping a wheel. The youngest and prettiest of the nuns took a break from her sponging to have a longer look at me.

Those nuns were wearing good quality religious gear – they were in their 'good' habits. In my monastery days, I had a work habit as well as a good habit: did these nuns not also have work habits? But perhaps they were in a hurry to set off somewhere.

I wore my work habit working on the farm of the monastery during my theology days. I was so unhappy that the black and white Collie who used follow me around took on my sadness and looked as miserable as I did.

As I left the nuns to their saintly car-cleaning, I realized with a tingle of the spine that I had actually lingered at the site of a church and my phobia had not clicked in. True, I hadn't gone *into* the church, merely admired the manual labour of the nuns in the forecourt. But perhaps, all the same, my phobia has diminished. It will have to, in a city where one cannot go a hundred yards without meeting a church of some kind or other.

If my phobia were to reassert itself, things could get really creepy here, surrounded as I am by saints and blesséds and blood-curdling frescoes of martyrs being martyred in various innovative ways and all the other relics of a past to which I once subscribed, for a whole chunk of my life.

I walked myself to exhaustion, losing my way and finding it again, then losing it once more. But I was determined to find The Golden Ass in advance, rather than leave it to chance on Friday. It was a sunny afternoon and I traipsed up and down Via Cavour searching for the restaurant. I called into an Irish bar called Finnegans, and the barman obligingly looked the restaurant up online and directed me to its street, which was Via del Boschetto. Having found the street address, I still couldn't find the restaurant. I accosted a man who was about to get into his parked car, but he said he'd never heard of it, then immediately exclaimed 'But here it is!'. The restaurant was beside his car. '*Che coincidenza*,' the man laughed and drove away.

Looking at the window of the restaurant, I saw that its name was a faint cursive frosting on a clear pane, obviously a transfer. Squinting inside, I thought I saw my father dining at one of the tables – the wide sweep of his broken elbow as he lifted food to his mouth: the break was botched by a bone-setter after he fell off a chair while checking a photographic light-meter in our back yard.

I looked again and this time the table was empty, the restaurant was empty, my father a trick of the light. There was a handwritten menu in the window and above it a business card which confirmed the chef's name was Lucio Sforza, the Orvieto chef recommended by The Rough Guide.

Later, coming back from a solitary pint in Finnegans, I passed a pavement-sleeper outside the Colosseum Metro. The sleeper was totally covered by a pink blanket or cloth which one raised knee had helped to assume the shape of an egg, as if he had disappeared back into the womb. A few meters further on, a crop of hawkbit flowers nodded on their green stems inside the railings of a park. These sights gave me the strangest inarticulate feeling: a mixture of sadness, joy, and an intuition of fate.

Rome is too full of churches. A rent boy is as likely as a saint to emerge from their shadows. The city is cluttered with the remnants of empires: the Caesars, the popes and now the outlets of multinational economic conglomerates appear in the sites where political and religious empires used to hold sway, and fashion shops are discreetly ensconced in the old buildings of Rome, while passé priests and toy legionaries walk around the streets among the jeans-wearing consumers.

Friday 05 November

I was expecting too much from the meeting with my old Roman friends. The Golden Ass was semi-deserted, although it was a

Friday night. The edition of The Rough Guide I consulted was probably out of date and the restaurant's popularity had waned. The food was good (all three of us had an excellent Umbrian dish of rabbit), but the conversation was awkward. Too much water had passed under the bridge since we last met. Not only that, but my Italian was far rustier than I had imagined. The whole business was something of a tooth-pulling.

There was a distraction, however, which rescued a smidgin of interest out of the evening. I met the distraction in the bathroom: a young man. He turned from drying his hands when I entered, looked me up and down, and muttered 'carino' as he brushed past. But he was the carino one, and more than carino; he was beautiful.

I spent the rest of the meal stealing glances. I was able to do that because of the enormous gaps in conversation at our table, during which we went at the Umbrian rabbit, muttering the occasional 'buono' or 'mmm' of appraisal.

The young man was sitting at a table quite close to us, with a heavy-set distinguished-looking white-shirted fellow who must have been close to sixty. The youth also wore a white shirt, but the sleeves had been cut off, exposing the loveliness of his arms. I noticed with some shock a detail: that his head was strangely – yet familiarly – shaven, a band less closely cropped circling his head between the more exposed spaces above and below it. A friar's tonsure, which in religious terms symbolized Christ's crown of thorns!

The mannerisms he displayed towards the older man were exaggeratedly camp, he laughed too loudly and was over-deferential. I thought: he's some kind of high-class rent boy.

Sunday 07 November

I met him again today. I had planned to go to the Pantheon but had to get off the Metro when I realized I had taken the wrong direction. I found myself coming out into a broad sunny piazza which contained a model of a pyramid, draped in scaffolding, a squat two-turreted castle which housed some kind of museum, fragments of ancient city walls, several bus terminals, an open-air café. I was thinking of going to study the bus and tram timetables, as I didn't like the idea of retracing my journey in the claustrophobic Metro, when I felt a pressure just under my shoulder blades. I turned, and was face to face with Beauty Itself.

'You should be more careful in the Metro,' Beauty said, holding up my wallet.

There was a twist of half-apologetic amusement on his lips. I was speechless, as much from meeting him again, my eyes drinking him in, as from realizing that he had stolen my wallet and was now giving it back to me

'It's really a bad idea to keep your wallet in your back pocket,' he said reprovingly. With another small shock, I recognized that his accent was Irish. He was wearing body-hugging jeans, a pink tank-top and a pair of sandals (in November).

'I know,' I said. 'I keep forgetting the dangers of Rome.'

He laughed. 'You were a sitting duck. But then I recognized you from The Golden Ass. Do you fancy a coffee?'

'Yes, yes. That would be...'

I looked towards the open-air café but he said, 'I live here, it's not far. Why don't you come to my apartment and I'll make you a proper coffee, not like the tar they serve in there? I feel I owe it to you for stealing your wallet.'

He slipped his hand under the crook of my arm, gently steering me away. How many of my birthdays are coming together? I wondered in a blissful haze, feeling the soft pressure of his hand.

On the short walk to his apartment, we exchanged first names and some small talk. His name was Hilary. He told me where we were, some very historic piazza. His pad was in a compound. He punched in codes at the gate and the main door. We took a lift to the second floor, where he opened a triple bolted door and let me in to a spacious living room with wooden table and chairs, a very conservative settee with green and beige stripes, a mustard-coloured television chair, a glass-topped coffee table, impressionist pictures on the walls.

'Enrico hasn't got much taste,' Hilary commented, 'but you don't argue when someone puts you up in such a spacious apartment.'

I felt a sudden sharp pang of jealousy at the mention of Enrico.

'He's the man I saw you with in the Golden Ass?'

'Oh well spotted, Martin! He's my keeper.'

'Keeper?'

'I can't think of a better name. But that's what he does, he keeps me. He has put me in storage here for his infrequent business trips to Rome. But enough of that for the time being. Coffee. Please sit down.'

I sunk into the armchair and Hilary went to the kitchen. Shortly, he was back again.

'While the coffee is brewing, I can give you a quick tour. Only if you're interested, of course.'

Hilary's kitchen was nearly as big as the living room, with a grey marble worktop. There were two bedrooms, a double and a single, and each of them had glass doors which opened onto a balcony overlooking a courtyard with young trees and tiled paths. My heart fluttered when he showed me the double bedroom, with its walls painted a light pink, and a huge double bed with wrought-iron bedsteads, a white duvet and long cylindrical pillows.

'The master bedroom,' I muttered enviously.

Suddenly, Hilary reached forward and kissed me full on the mouth, but as soon as I began to respond, he pulled away. I was shaking after his kiss. Again he put his hand in the crook of my arm and led me, sadly not towards the double bed, but back to the living room.

'Aren't you lovely?' he said. 'But I don't want to spoil things between us.'

I sat back in the armchair and calmed down. He arrived with the coffee, set it on the table and dragged the television chair closer. Why doesn't he sit beside me on the settee? I thought disappointedly.

'There's a few things I need to explain,' he said.

I had thought it likely that he wasn't being a shrinking violet during his master's absences from Rome, but I was shocked by what he told me. He assured me, at least, that he was very careful. But I recalled my own sordid visit to Spanky-poohs on the internet and found myself disposed to disregard his dark performances. And then he said something which thrilled me to the core.

'I don't regard you as just another conquest, Martin. You are special. I think I'm in love with you. There's something about you. You're so – *sound*. Soundissimo, in fact.'

'Pardon?'

'You know, *sound*. As they say back home, *a sound man*. I'm a bit of a flippertigibbet, but with you I feel grounded, safe. I can't explain it. I felt it straightaway back in the Golden Ass. And I couldn't believe it, when I realized I had robbed you, of all people, in the Metro.

'Of course I only saw your back at first, and there was your wallet actually protruding from your back pocket. It was so easy to remove it. You didn't notice a thing, you kept going. Then you must have realized you were heading the wrong way, and when you turned I recognized you. I followed you up to the street and gave you back the wallet only because I wanted to meet you again.'

'I don't know what to say.'

'Don't say anything. I want you to know that I'm sure we can be passionate together, in good time. But can we take this *pianissimo*? I have a strong conviction that otherwise it will all go up in smoke?'

'And what about your keeper?' I asked.

'I have a facility for dumping people I begin to find uncongenial.'

'That might apply to me too.'

'But that's precisely why I want us to have a softly-softly approach. I don't want to lose you, Martin.'

We kissed long and lingeringly before I left him. I wanted to do much more, but taking his advice, and with difficulty, I held back.

There was a spring in my step making my way back to the piazza, to resume my humdrum day so marvellously interrupted. I took a bus rather than the Metro. Not that the Metro hadn't been magically transformed in my mind, seeing that it had delivered my beautiful new friend to me.

I had never experienced such joy, not since the day Sarah said Yes, and I surprised myself, and probably some of the other bus passengers, by crooning snatches of old songs from my teenage years, like 'Daydream Believer' by the Monkees and 'I Can See Clearly Now' by Johnny Nash. Many of the commuters, on their way to resume work following the Mediterranean day's lunchtime hiatus, were smiling at me, and that monstrous monument in Piazza Venezia, the Wedding Cake as they aptly call it, seemed to express my elation.

That evening, I got a very sweet smile from a girl in a takeaway pizza joint on Largo Argentina, and we had a wordless joke about the way she picked up on her fork the tiniest piece of salmon that had fallen off my pizza slice and put it back on.

Dream of last night. I am being interviewed by a businessman. He sits by the side of a large double bed with a white duvet. He is heavy-set, wearing a white shirt, open at the neck, rather like Hilary's keeper. My wife is behind him, beside a large window, making querulous comments. I am extraordinarily reticent; I want to, but don't want to succeed. I am facing the interviewer, a few yards away from him. I do not see myself, I am just a presence. Well, obviously one doesn't see oneself, but it seems important for me to say this.

Later, I am accompanying the interviewer along a busy street, seeing him off, and talking much more freely. I shake hands with him before he crosses the street and feel relieved that he's gone, but I'm pretty certain that I've failed the interview.

This dream cast a slight shadow on my elation. I am particularly disturbed that Hilary didn't figure in it. Why is that, when he fills my entire waking consciousness?

(Later) The dream perhaps means that I will fail the 'interview' of my relationship with Hilary.

Wednesday 10 November

My elation slowly gave way to anxiety. The next morning I woke early, in a panic, realizing that we had made no appointment to meet again. We had exchanged telephone numbers, but a barrier, a high wall of fear, had been thrown up in my mind between me and the very idea of telephoning Hilary. It was too impersonal, too blind, too needy... too much a No-No. I needed to engineer a casual face-to-face meeting. But how could I do that, when I didn't know the name of the location where we met? My head had been too far in the clouds to enquire about it.

I knew, of course, that there was a pyramid and a castle with two towers. Taking several coffees in the breakfast room, I waited for the receptionist in the Borgo to arrive at nine, and described the place to her as best I could. She recognized it immediately as Piazzale Ostiense.

An hour later, I was in the Piazzale, seated at the open-air café I had seen before, doing a very different kind of people-watching than I normally do. I was surveying the commuters passing to and from the Metro, watching for Hilary. Hilary-Watching. I waited for hours, had a panino for lunch, a few glasses of wine. With the wine came a facile optimism, an inane conviction that, as fate had a hand in our first two meetings, so it would present a third one, because fated encounters are supposed to arrive in threes. With the fourth glass of wine, however, came the shattering counter-argument that a 'chance meeting' which had actually been contrived would not fulfil the requirements of fate.

Coming to my senses with a degree of self-directed anger, I rose, paid my bill and crossed the square in the hope of recognizing his apartment, knowing it was somewhere on the other side of the two-turreted portal, and not all that far away.

After about a quarter hour's futile wandering through a maze of streets, I saw a figure at an upstairs window, looking out. From its vague proportions, I was convinced that the figure was Hilary. I waved, but the figure closed the window.

Now I was convinced that Hilary didn't want to see me. Perhaps he was entertaining his business-man client from Milan? Or maybe he was with some other lover? Maybe he had many clients, many lovers? He had suggested as much to me. He's a total slut, I said to myself dejectedly – what a fool you are, wasting your time like this.

The building I stood before was a block of apartments, with the usual punch-in code required to open both the gate and the main entrance door. There was an intercom at the gate, but pressing the button produced only a prolonged crackling, then silence.

It was unlikely that the figure I saw at the window was Hilary: there was nothing left me but to phone. I took out my mobile and rang: immediately, a high-pitched female voice spoke strident Italian from the answering machine. The person at the number was *indisponibile*, it said – unavailable. I hadn't the courage to leave a message, couldn't trust myself to sound casual. I returned to the Borgo on the tram.

I was lying on my bed trying unsuccessfully to have my afternoon nap when my mobile rang. I leaped up and rummaged in the bed for my phone.

'Hello?'

'Hello, Martin. You rang me.' It was Hilary. He sounded friendly.

'Good to hear from you, Hilary,' I said, trying to contain my excitement. 'How are you?'

'I'm good. I've been thinking about you. A lot.'

'And so have I. About you, I mean.' There was a slight blurt-element in the way I responded, so I shifted direction. 'You know, I was in your area again today, visiting the Ostia Museum.'

'Not much of interest there, really.' I noticed that his voice was slightly slurred.

'No, no, rather disappointing really. But I had a wonderful view from the top of the gate.' I was using a detail from The Rough Guide to keep up my fiction. 'I tried to phone you afterwards, but there was no reply.'

'I had to switch off my phone on the plane.'

'Plane?'

'Yes. I'm in Milan. I was just ringing to say I'll be back at the weekend. I'd like to see you then. Very much.'

'Me too. When?'

'I've had a few drinks, Martin, I'm a bit blurry. Anyway I'll know more by Thursday afternoon. Can I phone you then?'

'I look forward to it.'

'*Alla fine settimana. Ciao, carissimo.*'

I tried to think of something sweet but not too giveaway in Italian by way of response to his *carissimo*, but he was gone.

Thursday 11 November

It is early morning, I am sitting in my spacious room at the Borgo, at the lacquered brown desk which is marginally too high for my chair. A mosaic-type painting of the Virgin or some female saint, with a church on fire in her breast, hangs on the wall to my left. Above her hangs a flat TV screen, which so far I haven't switched on. Behind me a small but exquisite chandelier suspends from the high ceiling. The walls are painted off-white. In one corner is a wardrobe and, straddling the other side of the room, the double bed where I slept very well last night, and woke with drowsily pleasurable thoughts of Hilary rather than my usual anxieties.

The window before me opens on a plot of garden with a few orange trees, autumn's fruit still plentiful on the boughs. There's a large bush of plumed bamboo to one side, and a path in the centre. It's an ideal place for a manifestation. So I'm hoping none of those figments that plagued my stay in Friesland, the Figure in Black or the Prophet of Doom, arrive on the scene to spoil my good fortune. I call them figments, and in my present state of happiness that's what they seem to be: the emanations of an unhappy and overwrought mind.

It is raining, as it has been almost every second day since I came here. I'm getting to like the constant sound of the screaming, scavenging seagulls outside the window. Sometimes it's like a witch's cackle, sometimes a hearty but cynical laugh, sometimes a dog barking (or is that an actual dog barking?). I hadn't associated Rome with seagulls, even though I knew from looking at maps that it was near the coast.

The receptionist here, Piero, is a polite and helpful man. He spoke to me of his son, who's a little older than my eldest (both in their teens), and complained ironically of how sons were always asking for money. He has a sense of humour, tinged with sadness, and a typical Italian cynicism. He has no problem lying to bureaucracy about his vintage car to avoid paying higher tax, declaring that he never uses it except to drive once a year to a vintage rally in Friuli. He surprised me once wearing motorcycle gear with a large helmet, looking like a spaceman behind the reception desk.

Andreina, the other receptionist, is a young woman, slim and pretty, in her twenties. She's diligent, cheerful, believes rather too much in what the internet tells her. Also she is very likely to inform you with great precision how to get to a place, without letting you know what an awful dive the place really is.

The Sleeper on the Pavement: I call him Abdul, the brown-skinned down-and-out I saw lying on the footpath across from the Colosseum. I imagine he composes seditious poems in Farsi, entirely in his head, as he lies there pretending to be asleep, then posts them to his sister in London to send to the US in English translation by email and social media.

I think when you're in love with someone, you are warmer towards other people. I love those three, the two receptionists and the pavement-sleeper. And I think I will always love them because they orbit around my meeting with Hilary.

I never wanted to end as a curmudgeon entombed in some home for retired monks. I never liked what people made of me when I wore the habit. I wasn't willing that they should idealize me (while at the same time denying me any individuality). There was so much I hated in their unctuous 'Ah hello, Brother Martin'.

I don't know what's happening to me here in Rome, after meeting Hilary: now, after almost fifteen years, it's become OK, overnight, if I see a bunch of monks in their cowls and habits in the street. In fact I experience an affection for the sight, and it begins (again) to propose something admirable to me, the unworldliness that betokens another way of life, another life. As long as I am not in there among them, part of the bunch, it's OK. Because I know after bitter experience that it's one thing to *see* a monk, another thing to *be* a monk.

I like to watch them, abruptly blown into sight by some mystic wind, in the middle of the crowded Streets, in the damp so-whatness, in Termini's teeming forecourt, jostled perhaps, but untargeted by pickpockets, a gaggle of giggling novices, excited at the prospect of a journey, long-bearded crusties in pairs as advised by the Holy Founder's Rule.

I couldn't take on that task of celestial signage myself; I was too internally messed up to correspond with the external image and felt the disparity too keenly.

And yet here in Rome, in love with Hilary, the sight evokes in me a sense of peace. I hope to God that my own religious order doesn't become implicated in this child abuse scandal. So far it has retained a clean sheet.

Dream in my afternoon snooze: I am talking with two attractive young women about the sights to be seen in various European cities. We speak in Italian and one of them mentions a 'Uomo con tridento' as one of the important sights in Rome. 'Uomo confidento,' I pun and we all laugh.

Obviously Freud would have made a meal of this dream, as a man with three prongs to his implement would certainly be confident in unconscious terms!

Friday 13 November

My second meeting with Hilary was not quite what I had expected. I had been building up the happy anticipation far too much and when he had not phoned by late evening yesterday, a miasma of impossibility had come down on my hopes, and my patience had collapsed. I rang him.

'Hello, Hilary?' I croaked. 'Is everything all right? I was expecting you to call.'

'You sound desperate,' he said. I was shocked by the frankness of the remark. Desperate, yes, spot on. Several penalty points incurred by my giveaway tone.

'Where are you staying?' he continued.

I gave him my address.

'I know it well,' he said. 'I stayed there when I first came to Rome.'

'How coincidental,' I mumbled.

'I'll tell you about it some time. There's a restaurant called Il Ristoro nearby. Do you know it?'

'I'll find it.'

'Good. See you in about an hour.'

The restaurant looked out on evening traffic and the imposing shell of the Colosseum. When I got there, a young woman was standing outside, touting for business. It was about half past seven, and the place was empty. I said I was expecting someone, ordered a Campari and orange juice, and to quell my over-excited mind, fixated a row of large bottles on top of a set of shelves in front of me, took out my notebook and wrote down the names of the wines: *Ruffino Riserva Ducale Oro, Chianti Classico Fontana Fredda, Barolo di Serralunga d'Alba, Barbero d'Asti Bricco dell' Ucellone....* These bottles were Magnums or Jeroboams and, as the young woman volunteered (having obviously glanced at my notebook), they were empty and purely *decorativo*.

There was something unnerving about the fact that she was the sole visible agent of this eatery, doubling as tout and waitress, and part of me was imploring unseen others to manifest themselves and prove the establishment's bona fide reality.

The Hilary that eventually turned up in Il Ristoro was not the Hilary I had met outside the Metro in Piazzale Ostiense. He arrived at about eight, tapped me on the shoulder, said a perfunctory 'Hi'. He was reluctant to sit down, rather he half-sat in the manner of someone who would soon go. He was in jeans, and the jumper he wore was some sizes too big, as if someone had lent it to him. But it was the look on his face that unsettled me most.

'I can't stay,' he said. There was something haunted about him, something alien in his features, and a cold tremor passed through me: he could never be mine, he belonged to some other realm of existence... He, too, was looking at me as if I was a strange being.

He lowered his voice: 'I need to be honest with you. I've been fucked senseless.'

I tried to maintain some display of decorum, what with the curious waitress restlessly coming and going between inside and outside, waiting for our order, and the surreal silence from the place's offstage departments

'Have you been.... raped?'

He laughed humourlessly.

'No. I put myself about a lot, Martin. I can't help it. It's an addiction. And drinking doesn't help. I was gang-banged.'

'I see,' I said coldly. 'And what do you expect me to say? *As long as you enjoyed it?*'

'That's the sad thing, Martin. I *did* enjoy it. That is, until it got nasty.'

'And you expect me to feel sorry for you?' I'm not a violent person, but what I wanted to do at that moment, instead of prolonging the conversation, was to break Hilary's jaw, shatter the alien look on his face.

'No, Martin, no. I don't want you to feel sorry, and I don't want you to help me. I just want you to understand the kind of person I am. That's all. I try to change, but I find myself getting into these situations without any conscious decision. Again and again. The way an alcoholic hears himself ordering a bottle of whiskey.'

'So that's what you want me for, to be your confessor?'

The taunt seemed to galvanize him. 'Allow me to repeat, Martin, and try to engage whatever few brains of yours are currently functioning: '*I just want you to know the kind of person I am.*' He stood up. 'I have to go. It's up to you. You can phone me or not later, whatever you decide.'

Numb, I agreed to the waitress's discreet recommendation of sea bream with baked sliced potatoes and salad, as if it were a cure for the pangs of love. I think she must have done the cooking herself, because she disappeared to the interior a number of times and after half an hour she came out with my fish. All the time I was there, I didn't see anyone except that young woman, who told me she was Romanian, and two new diners. I drank a bottle of wine, and found I wasn't totally dismayed by my contretemps with Hilary.

Sunday 15 November

On Saturday morning, I was spared a depressing comedown from the ersatz drink-induced optimism of my dinner for one at *Il Ristoro* by the tinkling of my mobile at nine am. The tone signified a text message rather than a call. Even though I dismissed it as surely coming from my network operator (they pester me with early morning texts, totally unaware of time zones), I got up because I knew I wouldn't be able to sleep any longer. I dressed and showered and had breakfast, with the intention of taking a trip back to Umbria, if my room there was still available: it would be a brief escape from the love-mess I was in. It was only when I was about to phone Oscar that I checked the text. It was from Hilary. *Please send email address. Will write. H*

I had mixed feelings about this message, delighted that Hilary had decided to maintain contact, but annoyed at the distanced way he was going about it. I knew I should get out of Rome to do some distancing of my own, so I phoned Oscar, and he was actually pleased at the prospect of my brief return. He even offered to collect me from the train. Probably a large part of me – the unconscious morass – was hoping he'd say No, he was fully booked, and I instantly regretted my decision. But I packed a small bag, took a bus to Termini, and after half an hour's queuing for a ticket, embarked on a train to Terontola, where my friend would pick me up.

As soon as the train jolted into movement, I felt good: *I* was taking control, *I* was setting down markers, not letting Hilary call the shots. I took great pleasure in texting him my e-mail address and adding *In Umbria for weekend.* Almost immediately came the response *Tnks. Enjoy xx*

The *xx* brought me a pathetic surge of happiness, the *Enjoy* gave me permission to forget my confusion for a while, to allow a chink of reality into the murk.

Orte, Attigliano, Orvieto, Fabro. The train trundled along unruffled by any sense of urgency. A cheerful man came through the carriage with two plastic bags, one of sandwiches, one of beer cans. I had a salami sandwich and a can of unchilled beer. Abandoned stations, crumbling signalmen's houses, desolate territory coasted by, until at last Lake Trasimene glinted in the winter sun.

At Terontola, there was an incident in my carriage involving a female ticket inspector and several ticketless youths. There were loud, angry exchanges, and the inspector eventually commanded them to get off the train. They did not leave easily, and blocked me in the aisle for several minutes. Repeated commands and threats were necessary and they finally descended, shouting recriminations and insults. One of them roared *Putana!* ('Whore!') and it was at this moment I saw Oscar arriving on the platform from the subway. He was embarrassed that I should arrive during such an unsavoury exchange.

On a sunny November day in Umbria, it is possible to sit outside for a few hours at midday, especially near a heat-reflecting wall. Oscar had arranged a trestle by the gable of the farmhouse, and we had a simple spaghetti for lunch with some white wine and bread.

'You look different,' he probed. 'If you'll forgive me for asking: has something happened you in Rome?'

This piece of curiosity opened my floodgates. and I told him all about my marvellous good fortune in meeting Hilary. As I spoke, however, I became unsure whether it was good fortune at all. A grey cloud of doubt seemed to settle on my spirits even as I enthused.

'You must send me a photo,' said Oscar.

'I'll send you a picture if I can get one from him. I don't think he likes giving out photographs.'

'How so?'

Suddenly, an image of Hilary flashed before me: his perfect knees, his beautiful thighs in clinging jeans, his svelte body, his cherubic yet mischievous face, the monk's tonsure on his perfectly moulded head, but above all I was assailed by love-starved tactile memories: of holding him and kissing him lingeringly that first time we met. Then the frustration of his keeping me at bay and advising me to take things easy resurfaced with angry frustration. I more or less flipped my lid in front of Oscar.

'I'm perfectly miserable without him, I said,' and suddenly burst into tears. And that bloody peacock, which was watching us from the roof, suddenly erupted in a fit of squawking, and Oscar lost his laconicism.

'Oh don't be such a sissy, Henry. You sound like a total twit.'

'I'm sorry.'

'Now might be the time to distract you with my piece of news. Yesterday, a woman called looking for you. In a Renault Megane.'

'A woman?' I whimpered. 'In a Renault Megane?'

'Yes Henry, opposite sex, woman, remember? French car, Renault Megane? And I think I saw someone else looking out from the front passenger seat, possibly a child, I'm not sure.'

'Oh my God,' I swore, 'there's only one woman that could be: my wife. What did you tell her?'

'You were in Rome.'

'Did you say where?'

'How could I? You haven't told me.'

'Don't tell her.'

'Fine,' said Mr Laconic. 'If you don't tell me, I won't tell her. Is that a bargain?'

'She never told me she was coming.'

'Well fancy that,' said Oscar. 'Imagine a wife not telling her husband that she's coming looking for him, to see what he's up to? What's the world coming to? Maybe I ought to have recognized her from before, but she wore dark glasses. I thought she might be one of your former acquaintances from that English crowd up in Umbertide. Pull yourself together, Henry, you're upsetting my peacock.'

But Oscar suddenly relented and placed his hand on my forearm.

'Henry, look at me. Surely you're not going to leave your wife for the sake of a little fling with a rent boy?'

'Oh Oscar, if only you knew how I feel about him. I love my wife but this is different. And I know in my bones that it's not just a fling.'

Oscar shook his head slowly. 'I have to say, I didn't think I'd see you so unmanned at your age. Something tells me it's make your mind up time.'

He rose and left me moping in the November sun while he collected dinner plates and things. Finally, he sat down again and lit a cigar.

'There's just one thing that bothers me,' I confided.

'And what is that?' Oscar exhaled a cloudlet of smoke.

'He keeps telling me I'm a good person, that it's what attracted him to me. And the truth is I'm fed up being a good person. I mean *Good* in inverted commas. I want to be bad if that's what

I'll be by having a liaison with Hilary.'

'What can I say? It's your life, Henry.'

And that bloody peacock squawked a loud affirmative kind of squawk, as if he agreed with what Oscar had just said..

6

SARAH

Sarah was a self-contained woman. No other kind of woman would have put up with Martin for very long. She worked for the Parisian Road Traffic Regulator as a clerical officer of intermediate status. She had a string of friends and was interested in all forms of art. She was petite, black haired, good-looking, and liked to dress in an avant-garde kind of way.

She was philosophical about her husband: when friends asked her where Martin was she'd reply, 'Oh he's just off being Martin'. Not that she didn't miss him but she had a strong perception of the person he was, a sense of his brokenness.

There *was* another side to her personality, that liked to punish Martin for his cavalier attitude of disappearing out of her life. She had made up the story of police calling to the house in search of him, and she had credited the fib with putting the cat among Martin's pigeons, causing him to leave Friesland for Umbria. But this was only half-true: it was Martin's belief that he was being sought by police from *two* jurisdictions, France and Holland, the idea of an *extending* manhunt, that had tipped the scales in favour of relocation. For no reason, as it turned out: the Dutch police were merely making routine enquiries about a drug cartel they suspected of beginning to operate in Sexbierum. The landlady, on the other hand, was simply horrified that any guest of hers, particularly a foreigner, should attract police attention.

Sarah relished the happy consequence of her proprietary prank: it was serendipitous in bringing Martin to Umbria, a region she loved for its art. Not only that, but the family had stayed with Martin five years before in the agritourist farm where he was now ensconced. She began to imagine a scenario in which she took the children on a cultural tour during the upcoming All Saints School Holiday, culminating in a family reunion.

But as her husband's phone calls became less and less frequent, his return date more vague, his replies as to what he was doing with his time even vaguer, and her own attempts to contact him more time-consuming and fruitless, her unflappable spirits began to wane and tetchiness started to take hold in her dealings with the children. She became less outgoing, less tolerant of the pointed enquiries her friends made about her husband. It was no longer easy to be flippant and say 'Oh he's just off being Martin'. Gradually 'off being Martin' didn't seem right: she was tired of his mealy-mouthed *Love-You* protestations on the phone from a distance of more than a thousand kilometers. She hadn't thought he'd stay away so long; she had a picture of him coming back after a few weeks with his tail between his legs.

Instead of being the life and soul of every party, she stayed at home in her leafy Parisian *banlieue*, watching television, doing puzzles and Pilates, waiting – as she told herself, *pathetically* – for a phone call from Martin.

She underwent a gradual awakening to life's precariousness, the fact that it could change and not in a good way, that the life she had, with its contentments and its *ding an sich*, might end. That there were sliding plates beneath her life. That the unconsidered life was hardly worth living, as someone had said. Or that her kind of unthinking existence and its acceptance and the identity it bestowed could reach a point of threat where you *had* to consider. Because everything would otherwise go downhill. And go more than downhill. And you had to do more than consider. You had to act. At this stage, she was no longer interested in arranging some sort of a tangential cultural tour, so that meeting Martin would seem secondary. She was only interested in confronting her husband, finding out what he was up to. She tested her plan with her office confidante, Ella, and the woman agreed wholeheartedly. *'Fais-le! Toute de suite!'*

Do it! Now! Sarah arranged to take leave from work for a fortnight, took her youngest child with her to Italy, and sent the two older ones to stay with her sister in Ireland for the All-Saint's Break, amid much protestation to which she responded with dark threats of 'You'll do this if you want to see your father again.' Which of course they did, because he was an easy-going Dad.

Mikey, more than the others, didn't want to leave home. Aged eight, he was homesick and car sick after a few hours driving and Sarah had to spend a night in a hotel in Villefranche-sur-Saone. She drank Campari at the bar while her somewhat recovered son played Gameboy on the room television after having burger and chips.

Next day they went over the mountains. Sarah's intention was to stay in a camping site she knew in Sisteron, where Mikey could be assuaged with a heated swimming pool and other amusements, but the campsite had closed for the year. Realising it was late in the year and not wanting to delay looking for another, Sarah drove on via Gap to Nice. Mikey, now more at ease with travel, admired the tires of trucks which were directly above their car on the snaking mountain roads. He tried to recognize cars which had gone from being *down below* to *up above*. He was also fascinated by the various sports cars and fancy coupés. Sarah, in the meantime, went through pangs of fear as she skirted abysses and swerved around bends.

Arriving late and tired on the city's outskirts, they booked into a pensione and went supperless to their room. Mikey was mollified by a bottle of Coke and a bag of peanuts from the mini bar. Sarah, relieved that they would arrive at Oscar's farm the following day, flopped into bed.

Late afternoon the next day, she drove up the dusty track outside Magione, overshot *Agriturismo Paradiso* to the next house, where she was redirected, only for Oscar to tell her that Martin had gone to Rome. And to add to her frustration, he hadn't been able to tell her where her husband was staying. He phoned a small hotel called Il Vecchio Granaio to book them in for something to eat and a night's sleep. He wasn't up to taking them himself at such short notice.

Arrived in Rome the next day, mother and son stayed in one of those quaint hotels where the ground floor was something different, and the reception and dining room were on the second floor with one or two more levels for bedrooms. But it was cosy and friendly, you could even order breakfast in bed, and a smiling dame with a hearty greeting would enter carrying a large tray of panini, prosciutto, salami, steaming coffee, pastries and confectionery, and place it gently on your bedcloth-covered lap.

Sarah wondered how she could dump Mikey for a while if she managed to locate Martin: the small hotel didn't supply child minders. At the very least, she didn't want him to witness the scene when and if she confronted his father. She had to discount the risk involved in leaving him to his own devices, but she took the long view that it was vital to find and have it out with Papa, so that the matter could be brought to an early resolution. Some kind of resolution anyway. And so, next morning when Sarah and Mikey were sitting up in bed having breakfast, she sounded out her son.

'Mikey, how would you like to go to Ireland like Shauna and Jim?'

'Only if you're going, Maman,' said Mikey. 'Anyway, I want to see Papa.'

'And if you stayed with me in Rome, and if I had to go to look for Papa, would you mind being on your own in the hotel until I came home?'

'Only if I can play Power Rangers and stuff, and watch Television and have a gelato after my lunch. But why do you have to look for Papa. Has he gone missing?'

'No, he has lost his memory. But it's all right, darling. His memory will come back when he sees me.'

'Well if that's the case, Maman, I shall gladly endure staying in the hotel on my own, playing Power Rangers, watching *South Park* and having two desserts a day.'

'You little imp!' Sarah gave him a pretend clip on the ear. 'And what is it you are most definitely not to do?'

'I am not to go anywhere with strangers. I may talk to them politely, but mustn't take anything from them like chocolate.'

'Good boy. I will introduce you to the receptionist so you can ring the bell or get her to phone me if you are bothered by anything or anyone.'

'Sounds like a plan.'

7

Martin's Rome Journal, Continued

Tuesday 17 November

N othing that I had admired and relished in the past about the farm, the town or the lake could lift my spirits on that forgettable few days in Umbria. Pub Franci's superlative pizzas in Magione tasted like paper in my love-hungry mouth. Likewise the marvellous *torta al testo* of the region and the radicchio roasted with olive oil and parmesan. The superlative *panna cotta* of a sheebeen on top of the hill above Oscar's agritourist venture was the only thing that came near a kiss from Hilary's lips, and that was a very distant, purely analagous closeness.

I drank red wine excessively on the Monday and was hungover earlier today, so that when the time came in the afternoon for my return to Rome, I was fit to be committed, a la my Prophet of Doom, to a psychiatric institution. Especially considering that I was torturing myself by refusing to look at three text messages which had dinged in my pocket in the course of my stay, any of which could have signalled the end of my affair with Hilary.

On the connecting train to Terontola, I teased myself about the possible content of the text messages, fantasizing desperate pleas from Hilary: *Miss you so much; love you madly, please come back*, and the like. I faced up to reading them only when I was snug in a half-empty carriage, on the Rome express.

But to my great disappointment and chagrin, there was no word from my androgyne beauty: two texts from competing service operators, and advance notice of my telephone bill. Then I was angry with myself for allowing Hilary's non-communication to upset me. For a long time I looked out broodingly, gloweringly at the dimming landscape of hills, hill towns and the winding Tiber.

Eventually, I persuaded myself that there was no reason at all for my distress: Hilary hadn't promised me a message, and at this very moment could be busy finishing his explanatory e-mail. My inner landscape regained some serenity as the outer one darkened. The train lumbered into Roma Tiburtina, last stop before Termini, and most of the passengers got off.

Back in my room, the first thing I did, without even taking off my coat, was to open my computer and check for e-mail. And sure enough there was one from Hilary. I read it with an increasing sense of shock:

ABOUT ME

I like being connected to men, Martin. I like it too much. When someone connects to me, and I mean in the plug-in sense, I know they fancy me, and that helps me fancy myself all the more. My life has been, so far, a continuous love affair with myself, as old Oscar Wilde (my favourite author) put it. But the unfortunate man who connects to me, well, he enters the centre of the universe, disappears down a black hole, he's gone and very quickly I connect to someone else.

I have to be truthful with you, I have looked at my ideal life as an ongoing gang bang, but a civilised one. It wouldn't turn nasty, not like what happened to me in Milan. It would have breaks for afternoon tea and scones with jam and cream.

Because I'm so good-looking, they are queuing up to fuck me, Martin. I survey them and I mentally assign them queuing tickets. It's like at Termini station, they wait around the ticket office until their number comes up. But for good people like you, when your number comes up at Termini, it's different, you go on a journey of your own choice, and when you get off the train, you're still the same person who got on. But people who fuck with me go on a journey that leads nowhere and lose themselves in the process. I'm a belle dame sans merci who leaves men palely loitering.

I know you'd love to ping me, Martin, like everyone else. But I strongly advise against it, because if you ping me, as sure as God you'll disappear into the black hole at the centre of my good looks. We can have cuddles if you like – and I'd like that too – but no heavy stuff. I cannot trust myself not to be promiscuous once the heavy pinging starts.

Reflection wasn't exactly part of my lifestyle up to now, but it has finally been forced on me. I need to think about Relationships and Responsibility, all that capital-letter stuff I despised. I need to sort myself out once and for all, or I'll end up dead, even murdered.

Milan was the last straw. They literally wrecked my ass, and that's another reason for not having any heavy stuff at present.

I hope you'll understand. If you can't cope without intercourse, at least for the time being, this will be my goodbye to you, because I couldn't bear to see you lose your identity, the good person you are, in the total confusion that is me. I would drive you under the ground.

There's more I need to tell you. But I can't e-mail it. I'd have to talk to you. That is, if you're still on board with me.

What could I do only cling to the slim prospect offered in that couple of redeeming phrases: *We can have cuddles if you like* and *at least for the time being?* My solitary existence in my cabin-febrile room suddenly oppressed me and I went out into the Roman night. I went to a restaurant I hadn't been to before, on Via Merulana, where the waitresses were dressed in lacy breast-lifting costumes like Alpine milkmaids and were more intent on their mobile phones than the customers. I ordered a bottle of Chianti Classico and had drunk it before one of them thought of handing me a menu. But I didn't feel like eating and ordered another bottle. Halfway through it, I plucked up the courage to phone Hilary. I didn't feel particularly sorry for him: his behaviour had been inviting sexual disaster. The principal emotion I felt, among many contradictory ones, was anger at being patronized by his monstrous vanity, but I knew that I had to sound sympathetic or I might lose even the possibility of cuddles. And if I could get once involved in cuddles, who knows...? Around the corner lay the whole hog..

Hilary eventually answered. 'I was trying to get some sleep after a very rough few days,' he complained.

'Sorry about that. I've just read your email, and I'd like to take up your suggestion of a little chat.'

'If you don't mind going to one of those all night places. It's getting pretty late.'

'Fine by me.'

'Ok.' He gave me the name and location of a gay night club near the Lateran. 'I'll see you soon as I can.'

'What were they saying to you?' I asked Hilary when we had found seats at a table in a relatively quiet corner of the bar. Hilary seemed to know several of the customers and had been mingling for a while when we first entered: he had just walked away from me as if I no longer existed.

'Oh the usual. Very flattering. How dishy I looked and all that. Several of them asked me out.'

'And did you assign them tickets?'

Hilary laughed. 'No, Martin. Don't be jealous now.' He drained his glass of wine. 'One of them asked me to dance. Do you mind if I do? It's just for the sake of form.'

'Don't leave me here too long. It's not really my scene.'

To the strains of a small band that could scarcely be heard above the din of talk all around, Hilary began to dance with a hulk of a man, bearded like Karl Marx, wearing a revolutionary greatcoat. The other drinkers moved aside to create space for the duet, and the music came over clearly as the talking stopped. It was some kind of Latin rhythm, a tango or a rumba. Pretty soon Hilary was up close and personal with his companion, reaching up his arms, stretching to link his fingers around the man's thick neck. The hulk placed his paws on Hilary's wriggling bottom.

The drinkers clapped and cheered. I experienced an intense pang of jealousy in the pit of my stomach, and wanted to intervene, but lacked courage, so I held tight and looked away.

When I looked again, Hilary had taken off his T-shirt, and was swinging it round and round to enthusiastic applause. His giant partner stood watching as he threw the garment aside. He took off the belt of his jeans, kissed it, tongued it lingeringly, ogling the bearded one, who snatched it from him and raised it above his head, holding an end in each hand, stretching it taut, being faux-masterful.

Hilary began to lower his jeans, edging them off slowly slowly, until at last they surmounted his splendid buttocks and flopped to the ground. I couldn't believe that I had been reduced to an incidental spectator of that wonderful golden ass in all its nudity, in an act of public indecency with a random co-protagonist, in front of a highly titillated mob.

Hilary now bent over, his dance-mate poised behind him. Total silence had fallen, even the music had stopped. 'You naughty, naughty, naughty boy!' roared the hulk, and raised the leather, now folded in two for greater impact.

The drummer played a sudden tattoo, ending on the *clunk!* of a dead note. The belt came down with a gentle smack on Hilary's rear. He pulled a face of saucy indignation, caressing his *as if* stricken part. Finally, to my relief, he hitched up his jeans, and bowed to the rapturous crowd.

The hulk handed him his belt and my wayward companion went off in search of his T-shirt. Dazed and humiliated, I suppressed my rage as he sat beside me, elated, flushed, waiting for my approval. Around us, the music and chatter resumed. I tried to play man of the world, the seen-it-all-before role.

'Interesting,' I said.

'You liked it?'

'Well, your ticket holders certainly did. And I'm sure you'll have a much bigger queue to deal with after *that* little display.'

Hilary laughed. 'Oh my poor little hothouse plant! You

should've been with me in Milan. Look around you. They're carrying on as if nothing had happened.'

'Having just read your e-mail, I thought you were about to reform yourself.'

'Oh Martin, you're such a prude. *That* was quite harmless.'

'Do you actually *know* that man you performed with?'

'Never met him before in my life.'

A barman came and handed Hilary a large glass of rosé wine. 'Very nice show,' he said. 'Very sexy. Would you like something, Meester? It's on the house.

'No thanks.' Irritably, I waved the barman away and said to Hilary 'We need to go somewhere quieter to talk.'

'That's fine by me.'

'Finish your drink, then. Back in a minute.'

Sometimes a full intelligible sentence will fall on the ear from a cacophony of competing voices, and on my way back from the toilet the following remark disengaged itself from the din and I heard it in complete clarity: *Il suo cozzo – é piccolissimo, l'hai visto?* (His dick is tiny – did you see it?)

We finished our drinks and Hilary made a big deal of his exit, going up to the bearded one and kissing him on the mouth, waving and wiggling his way to the door. Most of the customers cheered and applauded once again, but I thought or maybe imagined I caught the love-starved gaze of a few who watched him go.

> *I saw their starved lips in the gloam*
> *With horrid warning gapéd wide...*

'I can't understand why you would want to embarrass me like that,' I said. We were nighthawks in a late-opening café near a bus park from which several routes took off.

'Oh for God's sake, Martin!'

'I mean, that brute you were dancing with. What on earth did you see in him?'

'Do you want me to be frank with you?'

'Yes of course.'

'It's all to do with *size*, Martin. Big man, big cock: that was my take on it. If you weren't there, I'd have gone off with him for the night. I like big in the penis department.' Hilary chuckled.

'Maybe it's compensation, seeing how tiny your own dick is.'

His face fell. 'Martin, that remark is below the belt.'

'Well chosen words. Apparently, you know all about being below the belt.'

'Ouch! That, too. Below the belt, beneath the cock. Sodomy and S&M have been my favourite sports. But you're right: my dick *is* tiny. Hardly a dick at all. But that's irrelevant to my modus operandi. My orgasm is internal. I'm sure you've gathered by now that I am a penetratee, not a penetrator.'

'But you won't hear of *me* penetrating you. Oh no.'

'I didn't say that, darling. I just advised against it, for a while.'

'And what if I want to, what if I cannot look at you without wanting to…?'

Through the window, I could make out the thirteen or fourteen illuminated statues on top of the Lateran cathedral, apostles and patriarchs, sound men all of them, who wouldn't yield an inch to the temptations of earthly beauty.

'It's nice that you want to, I'm very flattered. And I *could* do with some serious cuddles. But I still think the old actual sodomy should be avoided for the present. I'm inclined to be very reckless and stupid after getting heavily pinged.'

'Until you're reformed, of course. Then it'll be all right for me to give you a length or two I suppose.'

'Yes.'

'As if,' I sneered.

'Don't knock me. And please, *please* don't jump to the conclusion that tonight's little show is proof that I'm beyond reform.'

'Why shouldn't I? You didn't have the decency to sit with me even for a few minutes, before you were off after your giant of the disproportionately large member, indulging a fantasy you would have fulfilled if I hadn't been there.'

'But that's the whole point. Normally, I would have gone off with Bulkykins and left you holding your willy. But something told me I mustn't mess with you, Martin'

'But you *did* mess with me.'

'I'm sorry if you see it that way. But look at it from my point of view: having been a flippertigibbet for so long, I feel I behaved rather like an angel tonight.'

I had to admit to myself that Hilary was earnest, also that I had no idea what depths he was emerging from, in comparison to which his performance in the gay bar might be considered angelic.

'So what happened you in Milan?'

'I'll need another drink before I can tell you that. But to tell you the truth, Martykins, I'd like to go home. We can take the night bus – it's not far.'

I bought a bottle of wine and we boarded a bus for Piazzale Ostiense. Hilary sneaked his hand into mine as we sat together, and leaned over to whisper in my ear: 'Can't we just go to bed?'

That night in bed together was rather awkward and inconclusive. I hadn't had sex with anyone for ages, at least ten years, and that was with a my wife. I hadn't had sex with a male before Hilary, although I had begun to fantasize about it. But my body seemed to be anaesthetized against sexual pleasure as Hilary snuggled into me that night.

As we lay together in naked embrace, he said 'This is very friendly.' A new connotation of the word, as far as I was concerned: I thought we had gone beyond friendship by bedding one another.

I touched him up and down, felt every part of him, and he was lithe, lissom, strong, flexible, snake-like, firm and undulating, silky, downy, eagerly writhing against me. I kissed him for world-record durations, he stroked my penis, tugged my penis. All remarkably to no avail. He was very patient and understanding, the young teacher explaining to the older pupil that it takes time for bodies to attune to one another, and my nit-picking head wondered did he ever stay with anyone long enough for their bodies to attune.

We slept fitfully that night and had unremarkable cuddles again the next morning.

Afterwards, we sat up in bed together, drinking Earl Grey, which is Hilary's favourite tea and coincidentally also mine. To me this particular brew seems to have the taste of sweet fornication, because an early girlfriend of mine served it to me in a house near King's Lynn after a blissful night we spent together. And although Hilary and I had just spent a fairly horsey and not very comfortable night together, that's neither here nor there: the taste of Earl Grey has become fixed in my mind as the taste of sex, and was now associated not only with my partner in King's Lynn but with the feel and the taste of Hilary.

'I wanted to ask you something, Martin,' Hilary began after a few moments of appreciative tea-sipping. 'What on earth did you mean by *the way you half-incline*? Remember – that was one of the phrases you used last week when I asked you what you found attractive about me?'

There was a tiny clink as he put his cup down on his saucer, then silence. A tingling of morning light came into the dull room from around the edges of the window shutters.

'That's a hard conundrum,' I said at last. 'But let me try and explain... It's like your every gesture seems to signal an in-between-ness. As well, of course, as a willingness to come over, which I find infinitely more arousing than the ostentatious behaviour of lots of gays.'

'Go on.'

'Also, your *body* is already a presence, an erotic presence, before *you* do anything. It is already tantalizing beyond belief. *To what serves mortal beauty – dangerous; does set dancing blood* – and so on. Hopkins. Then *you* come along, in there in your body, with your unconscious aura of *will-I-won't-I?* Well it's not even as definite as that. It's just a *slight* hint of possibility that you emanate.'

'But it all ends up so sordidly if I do, doesn't it?' Hilary said. 'When you ping me, I lose what attracted you to me in the first place. It's a paradox. You'll be left with nothing but sperm and smells – and arguments and rows. Isn't that true?'

'Other people may not notice it, but it is my blessing and curse to notice that you are a beauty apart, of mind in body, body expressing mind, mind-body, boy-girl, woman-man. You are the bodily expression of the Kabbalah in person.'

'To you I am Dorian White. But I can easily become Dorian Black, or just plain old smelly Dorian Gray.'

'I feel that you are so delicately balanced,' I said, 'so on the cusp - and that is your nature and nurture. It was lovely to have held you, to be with you, to make love to you gently. Surely it would not upset your balance too much to go the whole hog?'

'Martin, I am absolutely convinced that going the whole hog with you at the moment would turn me into a fallen angel. – OMG!' Hilary laid his cup on the bedside locker and jumped out of bed. 'I'm late for work.'

It came as a surprise to me that Hilary had to go to work at eleven o'clock on Monday. Apparently he had landed himself a part-time job, three half-days a week, as a supervisor in the Keats and Shelley Museum by the Spanish Steps, a post which very simply involved keeping an eye on the exhibits and the visitors.

'Not that the visitors, on the whole, get up to anything,' he explained. 'They're usually very keen Keats and Shelley fans, academics, poets and so on. But you never know when some nefarious person might slip in and try to nick something valuable, like a cartoon from an old issue of *Punch* or a first edition of one of poor Keats's hostile reviews. Or even in the hope of robbing the till of its pickings.'

We agreed to have dinner together tonight and parted with a quick kiss at the entrance to the Metro.

Slowly with the growing day, my body's delayed reaction set in. Something beautiful had happened to it. By the time I got to my digs, my skin was singing from every pore.

Tuesday 17 November

Dinner date cancelled. It seems that some other Bigwig (not his keeper) has invited Hilary to Milan for some sort of orgy-cum-catwalk in a country mansion. It's called a *Bunga Bunga*, he says. He also told me that his keeper had heard of certain Roman infidelities. The nasty gang-bang was a kind of revenge.

'So you're off to Milan again. Just my luck.'

'Don't be down about it,' he says. 'I'll be careful. Anyway, this guy is a politician, he's not like Enrico, he won't risk scandal. My feelings for you make me all the more determined not to overdo it. Don't you remember what I said first time I saw you?'

'*Carino*,' I said.

'Yes!' says Hilary. 'That was sincere, you must accept that it was my gut feeling the very first time I saw you, in the WC. You are such a nice person, Martin.'

But I don't want to be such a nice person, damn it!

8

SARAH ON THE TRAIL

At first, Sarah thought she'd have to compile a list of possible places where Martin could be hanging out – hotels, pensioni, hostels. It was too daunting a task to cover every lodging in Rome, and so she had to ask herself what sort of establishment Martin was most likely to stay in. She knew that he liked plush hotels, but he would probably avoid them at present, given that his decision to take a break from teaching ruled out lavish spending. On the other hand, he wouldn't go for dosshouses. There was always the slight possibility that he was staying with a friend, but he hadn't many friends. She felt he was more likely, loner that he was, to opt for a less socially demanding retreat. Especially if he had society enough in someone with whom he was being unfaithful.

She was aware that Rome was full of relatively cheap places to stay, many of them run by the Catholic Church, but she didn't know of any. She felt that Martin, as a former monk, would know some of those or know how to get information about them. And then it struck her like a bolt from the blue: why not ask the Irish Embassy had they a list of moderately priced locations. They had.

It took her a couple of days, between her own exhaustion and prolonged trips to satiate Mikey's boredom, to hit the jackpot at Borgo Irlandese, the twenty-first name on the non-alphabetical list the Irish Embassy sent her. She phoned and asked for Martin.

'Hmm, name sounds familiar,' said the receptionist. 'Let me see.'

Sarah's heart ached with tension as she waited for the receptionist to check.

'Yes, there's a Martin Kelly staying with us at the moment. He was originally due to leave yesterday but he has extended his stay for a further month.'

Aha! I've got you, Mr Moonlight, thought Sarah.

'Thank you. May I speak to him?'

The receptionist tried the extension. 'I'm sorry, there's no reply at the moment. Shall I leave a message?'

'No thanks. I'll try again later.'

Sarah waits outside the Borgo in the morning rain, buys a black umbrella from a cheerful street vendor on Via dei Santi Quattro. To mesmerise her mind away from what she's doing, she watches the sailing boats of rain splash around her in a crowded regatta. Then she spots Martin coming out the Borgo gate, turning left towards the Colosseum. She follows him, breaks into a trot. They both get on the Metro heading towards Termini, in adjoining carriages. Having stood at the door of her carriage watching for him, she spots him leaving the carriage in front. She trails him to an area with multiple signs for tickets, sees him detach a queuing ticket from a dispenser, having brushed off one of the 'expert advisers' who abound at the station. He stands nervously where he can watch for his ticket number and ticket desk to come up on a monitor. Sarah sizes up the system, grasps that he has to stand around for a while, and that now is the time for her to pounce.

She walks up to him and says, 'Hello Martin.'

'Sarah!'

Martin drops his queuing ticket and it spirals downwards on to the floor like a winged sycamore seed. Recovering a little from shock, he hams it up with 'What a pleasant surprise.'

'We need to talk, Martin. Is there anywhere we can go?'

Martin leads her, both of them silent, to the nearest station bar. He orders an espresso, she asks him to bring her a glass of water. When they have settled at a table, Sarah says 'What's all this about, Martin?'

He endures a spell of inability to speak, finally goes for broke. 'I met someone.'

'You *met* someone? You don't mean you're having an affair, do you?'

'Yes.'

'And who with? Who is she?'

'Not a woman. A man. Hilary is his name. A young man. He's beautiful and I'm totally in love with him.'

Sarah broke into tears and he was suddenly ashamed. She was the one person in the world who had let him be himself and lived with him over the years and bore him children, not making many demands, who always had that easy tolerance and affection, knowing him as a bit of a doo-dah and space cadet and yet, somehow, at home with him. Now that he had walked away from their at-homeness together, he could see in her tears how his desertion had breached the barriers she had against the perilous open spaces that would invade her, making her part of the general chaos and the world's unhappiness. He saw fleetingly that the happy spark of her spirit could be extinguished, that he would be the one who extinguished it, that she would become someone else, embittered in that elseness. He saw clearly for the first time the wreckage he was wreaking.

'I'm sorry I've hurt you so, Sarah,' he said. 'I'll call it off and go home with you.'

She dried her eyes with a paper napkin and said 'You bloody well better. How in God's name did you allow this to happen?'

'It just happened, Sarah. I didn't plan it. He stole my wallet on the Metro and then recognized me from the time I was having dinner with Claudio and Claudia at the Golden Ass and he was having dinner at the next table with his keeper...'

'His *keeper*?'

'Yes, Sarah. Hilary is a sort of high class rent boy.'

'Martin, this is a side of you I cannot deal with. How do you know you haven't picked up some awful venereal disease?'

'Firstly, because Hilary is high class and his minder insists that he takes all precautions. Secondly, because we haven't had intercourse.'

The look of relief on Sarah's face irked Martin a little bit, so he added 'We *have* slept together and cuddled one another, like the Old Christians used to do until the Church put a stop to it. But Hilary wanted us to have a softly softly approach because he thought early intercourse was unwise...'

'Imagine that! How careful and intelligent of him! And you, of course, were actually keen on going the whole hog?'

'As it turned out, that wasn't advisable. His bottom had been wrecked in a gang-bang, Sarah.'

'Aw Bless! The poor little devil. Right, Martin, this is it! Either you give up your rent boy or we're finished.'

'I've had my fling, Sarah. It's over, I swear.'

'I want you to put an end to your anal adventures and come home, right now, to me and your children.'

'Sorry, Sarah. I need to say a proper goodbye. It's only right. It wasn't all about sex.'

'No way, Martin.' Sarah rose to go.

'You can witness it if you like. I can say goodbye to him in public and you can watch discreetly. How about the Spanish Steps?'

Sarah was tempted by the prospect of seeing the little rat who threatened to take her husband away from her, and succumbed.

'All right. As long as the two of you behave. And make it quick. Otherwise....'

'It'll be absolutely kosher, Sarah.'

They rose and walked out of Termini, neither of them sure what they felt, overwhelmed by the stress of their conversation, dithering in the rain.

Eventually, Sarah said, 'And now, Martin, how would you like to see your youngest? He's waiting at the hotel. I managed to get the receptionist to look after him. Your other two children went to Ireland for the All Saints Holiday, and they're home now. God knows what they're up to. What in the name of God came over you?

'What can I say, Sarah?'

'Nothing. We're heading off on Monday, and I need you to help me with the driving. Today, you can bring Mikey to see the Colosseum. We'll keep the talk till we get home.'

A very chastened Martin, who had intended travelling all the way to Milan and Hilary that morning, went to meet his son Mikey instead.

9

HELLO AND GOODBYE

There was a man sitting at the bottom of the Spanish Steps as Martin approached them. He was bent slightly forward, head erect, looking straight at nothing. Staring nothing in the face, and letting the world know. In the ninth of the nine circles of fed-up-ness. Making a silent public statement.

In his late forties, grey-haired, grey-bearded. There was a hood on his dark jacket, but he hadn't pulled it up. Rain splattered gently on his bald head and on the Spanish Steps.

Martin caught a glimpse of two members of the Polizia Roma higher up, smoking cigarettes, perhaps keeping an eye on the man who wanted the world to know. He continued up the steps, conscious of the gravitational pull of Hilary's presence in tight jeans and top, his darkly tonsured head. It was as if he had created a miniature black hole right in the centre of the iconic place. He's getting more alluring as he gets wetter, Martin thought, again recalling Coleridge's lines from The Rime of the Ancient Mariner: *He holds him with his glittering eye.* But it was more the case that Hilary was holding him with his glittering everything. This is going to be awful, he thought.

'Why are we meeting out here in the rain and cold?' moaned Hilary. 'It's not good for my complexion and I could catch my death.'

'Hilary, I've met you here because my wife is watching. I'm leaving you, and she wouldn't allow me to say goodbye without being able to witness it.'

'So she found you, Henry? Clever girl! Oh well, *c'est la vie*.....'

'Is that all you have to say to me? *C'est la fucking vie?*'

'Why is it that because I look this way rather than another way, that I'm a good looker, a *really* good looker rather than having looks that are ordinary or even plain ugly, that men can't get over me or out of me? I genuinely thought you might be my saviour, but now I see we're dealing with competing salvations, that it's either me or your marriage. That's probably why I said *c'est la vie*. So it's huggies and go rather than huggies and stay. Goodbye, Martin. You see, I cannot guarantee you permanence.'

'Fuck you and your absence of permanence.'

'Fuck you and your absence of availability. But I'll always remember you.'

'And me you.'

They hug. 'Where is she?' asks Hilary, gaping around as far as the hug allowed. 'Can I have a shufti?'

'Don't push it.'

'I really can't stay here getting soaked, Martin. Stay in touch.'

The man sitting at the bottom of the Spanish Steps seemed like one of those performers who are perfectly still, miming a statue, except he hadn't the silvery-grey make-up. As Martin approached, the statue suddenly came to life. An arm reached out, a hand raised two fingers in bored regal impatience. The gesture was halfway between asking for a smoke and downright rudeness.

It was the last straw for Martin, to be given a V-sign by this haughty scrounger, who reminded him of the con man he encountered on his first day in Rome.

'And fuck you too!' he retorted, bringing the curtain down on his stay and his recently developed penchant for choice language.

Hilary went back to the Keats Museum, where a colleague advised him to go home and change. And Sarah, under her recently purchased large black umbrella, came forward from her vantage point, and walked to the Metro with her regained husband.

Never, now, will you ride your sleekit horse to Pingdom Come. It was like when you've been listening for twenty years and in the end you begin to hear what a person is saying to you, the voice of the person inside, and how it belongs to you and why you chose her though you didn't know why you stuck with her. Or why she stuck with you. There was something that held you in her voice, in her comportment — the way she held herself held you, the still small voice insistent over all.

10

PHONECALL

Martin had seen the eternal footman hold his coat and snicker. He returned to being Martin of old, but with some modifications. Back teaching in Paris, he had a substantial amount of Brownie Points to garner before things returned to normal at home. But he went about collecting them like a man. He also took on hobbies such as Round-the-clock Golf (with Mikey) and making model boats. Sarah returned to work and got back into her social and artistic circle. Once or twice a week – a new development – the two of them watched television serials together.

One wonderful thing Martin began doing, when he returned to teaching, was to foster a deeper appreciation of poetry among his students at the Lycée, despite opposition from the Head of Literature Studies. He eventually won his superior over somewhat, having convinced him that the students, who were intelligent enough to do so, would keep his new way of approaching poetry off their exam scripts for two simple reasons: first, it couldn't possibly get onto an exam script; and second, that they wanted to pass their exams. And so, like the workers laid off from Jacob's Dublin factory in relation to the mystery of how figs got into fig rolls, Martin's students would bring with them to the grave the new intuitive way of appreciating poetry they had acquired, of seeing its eternal fruits in their temporal integuments.

Only one thing remained from that seismic November: a recurring dream of mist, of a fog in which Hilary appeared and disappeared, approached and receded through the swirling wreaths. Martin would wake from the dream sitting up in bed, his arms outstretched, feeling a loss that was physically painful, a desperation. But Hilary eventually disappeared from the dream, leaving nothing but the swirling mist, and no reason whatsoever for him to reach out his arms. Except towards his sleeping Sarah as he gently strokes her hair. Aboard his sturdy living-in machine, sailing towards evening in a Parisian suburb.

And then, one morning in mid-December, Martin received a phone call: 'Hi Martin, it's me. Hilary.' He stared wide-eyed at the screen of his mobile, at the forbidden number.

'Uh.., hello Hilary. Where are you ringing from?'

'Paris. I'm staying overnight with a friend near the Bastille. I'm on my way to London. A flight at five. I presume you are familiar with Porte Maillot? The pub at the pick-up place for the bus to Beauvais for Ryanair flights to Ireland? It's called the James Joyce. I am on my way to London and I could meet you there and then pop over to Charles de Gaulle for my flight. I thought it might be a nice idea for us to meet up.'

'I do know it, and what a very nice idea indeed. Time?

Oh around lunchtime. Half-Twelve?'

They drank beer on high chairs at an external trestle under an awning outside the Canadian Embassy Pub (the new name for The James Joyce) in a narrow street with parking spaces for scooters and motorbikes across the way. It was quite crowded inside, with early revellers, and people returning to Ireland from Beauvais, waiting for the bus. Hilary plonked his rucksack on the ground beside his stool and had a difficult job sitting. 'I've had a pingholectomy,,' he said. 'Ouch! Anoplasty, you know? No more pinging for me.'

'I'm really sorry,' said Martin, thinking *He looks as beautiful as ever.* 'I do hope you don't need a cholostomy bag or anything annoying like that.'

'Luckily, No. And Enrico has cashiered me. Left me a tidy sum, though. No more rent boy for me.'

Martin suppressed a grim satisfaction because of the equality the news conferred on them: his own gallop, too, had been halted, not by an Anoplasty, but by his wife.

'I'm sorry that they messed you up so, Hilary. How are you taking it?'

'As a sign from heaven of course.' Hilary grinned. 'But you may remember me saying that I needed to take stock of things?'

'I remember it very clearly.'

'Well, I'm beginning to consider old Hamlet and his spiel about the divinity that shapes our ends. I've met someone....'

'Not a case of another stolen wallet?'

'No more of that. In fact, it's not a man, it's a woman. I'm going to London to be with her for a while. She's studying at Goldsmith College.'

'I don't believe it.'

'I always thought I was hard-wired gay until I met Francoise. I think the chemistry between two people must be a lot more mysterious than is imagined.'

'Indeed. But why are you in Paris rather than taking a flight from Rome to London?'

'A mix-up, Martin, I'm very good at mix-ups. I thought she was coming back to Paris rather than me going to London. And you, Martin? How are things with you?'

'Actually good. I'm heaping up the old kudos to make up for my transgression. Sarah has been very OK about it. She's an angel.'

'And are you happy?'

'Now that pinging you is totally out of the question, I'm happy with Sarah and my kids. And also more relaxed. What will you do in London?'

'Catch up with Francoise. Have you been to London, Martin?'

The question brought back Martin's memory of his arrival in London, having left Ireland and his Dublin monastery. He looked at Hilary's tonsure, thought of the times he had kissed his head, and could not bring himself to mention his cloistered days.

'During the recession in the early eighties, I was unemployed and went to London in search of a job. Of course I had no problem getting one in a London Catholic School, they were short of teachers and it was enough to have a BA at the time. But things were too tense for me on account of the bombings, with shopkeepers flinging my change at me across the counter on account of my accent, and other forms of hostility. So I collected my two years' pension from teaching and went to Paris, where I met Sarah at a do in the Irish Embassy and eventually got a job in a Lycée. Jesus, it's only now we're talking about backgrounds. Everything was so helter-skelter in Rome.'

'And you were after only one thing, Martin.'

'Indeed. And probably still am. As it is, I can't take my eyes off you. If someone asked me to describe our present surroundings, I wouldn't be able.'

'I'm a very fluid sort of person, Martin, but here goes. A little keepsake.'

Hilary leaned forward on his seat and caught Martin with a prolonged smacker on the lips. Martin responded hungrily, his hands reaching down and under Hilary's shirt. Incongruously, a woman came past them on the way out, wheeling a child in a pram. A man followed, wearing a hoodie, speaking to the airwaves. Martin pulled away.

'You couldn't make it up,' he said. 'A timely reminder of my marital status. I read a book about Shakespeare which said that when he came back to Stratford from London, Anne Hathaway was actually able to *see* the caresses of women on his body. Enough is enough.'

'Ah yes, Sarah, of course. I remember watching the two of you walking past the Keats' Museum, under that big black umbrella, and thinking *Poor Martin*.'

Stung, Martin threw back, 'Cheek! Staying with you, I would have been Even Poorer Martin.'

'*Touché!* Time for another?'

'Not for me. Have to drive.'

Hilary found himself engaged by an admirer inside the pub,

and Martin was tapping his fingers nervously on the trestle by the time he came back.

'Another fan. Tell me Martin, was there anything about me that you found particularly attractive? Apart from that Will-I-won't-I stuff you mentioned before. Excuse my vanity, but it's a question that always intrigues me.'

'Surely, Hilary, you've realised by now the whole point of being a stunner is that there's nothing in particular that's attractive. It's the wholeness that counts.'

'Is that some kind of pun?' Hilary tittered.

'Very funny. I mean the wholeness of your physical being. It's also the harmony of all your different bits and pieces, and above all the radiance. In your case, the radiance comes from being admired so much, being loved and made love to so much. *The roses had the look of flowers that are looked at.* It's the radiance of your self-complacency, your self-love.'

'I can see that you studied more than your prayers.'

'Yes, I did. I studied philosophy as well as English at college. And I've also had a lot of time for reflection since last November. But there's another aspect to bodily beauty, the urge it provokes. *To seize and clutch and penetrate*, as Eliot put it – the desire to possess, jealousy. On the other hand, aesthetic appreciation and benevolent love do not arouse desire, they are focussed on the *ding an sich*, disinterested – which is not the same as being uninterested.'

'Easier said than done, Maestro.'

'Yes. It's the old difference between Eros and Agape. A poet once expressed the superiority of Agape in a pun – Eros staring agape at Agape.'

'You know, Martin, I kind of actually get what you're saying and it makes me feel good. It makes me think of what I felt for Francoise when I first met her at an exhibition in the Pompidou Centre. I don't know how it relates to what you've been saying, but it was a very strong sense that there's more to love than sexual attraction. The attraction was there but there was more, a feeling of coming home, of being there, of being plucked out of the morass…'

'Interesting word, plucked. St Augustine used the same word about his conversion: *O Lord, Thou pluckiest me out…*'

'I felt something the same when I saw you in the Golden Ass. But you were on a different planet then, the Planet of the Apes.'

'Well you weren't exactly a Seraph yourself.'

A man of colour, hawking bling and baubles, and some single roses, the stems wrapped in foil, approached them.

'Where you from, guys? Ireland?'

Martin gave him a few coins for a rose, and gave the rose to Hilary.

'In memory of our lost Eros and to our new-found Agape.'

'Thank you, Amen,' said Hilary, and kissed him on the cheek. Chastely.

Martin looked at his watch. 'I need to get back to domestic bliss. And you need to make a move to catch your plane.'

They parted. Martin went to the toilet and as he came back out of the bar, he spotted a waiter clearing glasses from where they had been sitting..

'This is yours, Mister?' he asked, pointing under the table.

In a state of shock, Martin mumbled an apology and took Hilary's bag from where it lay on the floor and checked it. He discovered his friend's passport and boarding pass in a side pocket of the bag. And in the other side pocket, he found a mobile phone. He waited for half an hour at his seat in the hope that Hilary might return. Surely he'll come back, he thought; he'll have to. But Hilary did not return.

Driving home from Charles de Gaulle Airport, Martin fumed and cursed his luck. He had left a message on Sarah's phone, also on his daughter Shauna's, to say he had been delayed and would be back before dark. But given that he had rarely ventured very far since returning from Italy, he knew he was in for scrutiny. He had been too annoyed with Hilary to page him after the trying experience of the crowded airport; instead he got the PA system to announce the rucksack, and left after giving it in.

Eventually he arrived in the door, braving it out with 'Hello, my Lovelies.' He was touched when he saw that they had all been sitting on the big sofa, watching television and waiting for him: an uncommon togetherness.

'Martin!'

'The wanderer returns!'

'Dad!'

'PSG beat United, yay!'

The children immediately deserted the sofa and went to their rooms, to play with their phones or tablets before bed.

'Are you hungry, Martin? I can heat something up for you.'

'No, I'm fine, Sarah, thanks.'

'It's Hilary, isn't it?'

'Spot on. He phoned me this morning that he was in Paris and could I meet him. He's got a girlfriend, imagine. She's French.'

'Really Martin? Has the leopard changed its spots?'

'Oh come on, Sarah,' Martin retorted, and echoed Hilary's remark from their conversation at Porte Maillot: 'The chemistry between people is more mysterious than we know.'

'I'm not particularly worried about Hilary and his seeming conversion to straight. What bugs me is why you should dash off and see him purely at his beck and call.'

'Because I value his friendship, Sarah, as I told you before. And I was delighted to hear from him. I was also relieved that he wanted to meet me simply for a chat.'

'So there was nothing else between you?'

'Well, to be honest, Sarah, he did make a lunge at me and kissed me. Just once. But I pulled back. He admits he's still very fluid.'

'And are you still fluid, Martin?'

'Isn't that what's coming to the surface these days, Sarah? That we're all fluid, in various degrees. But I really believe he's had a Road to Damascus experience. Even in Rome, he was talking about having to rein himself in.'

'You haven't answered my question, Martin.'

'Obviously I'm fluid, Sarah, as I confirmed during my travels. But I also discovered during my travels that I'm not fluid about my love for you. *That* is a no-brainer.'

'Well, I wouldn't want to deny you a friendship, Martin. As long as that's what it is. So his latest is a French girl?'

'Yes. She's studying something or other in London.'

'I hope she's good for him and he doesn't dump her. Go to bed, Martin, you look wrecked. We can talk again tomorrow..'

Martin went up the stairs. At the top, he raised his joined hands in thanks.

Sarah sat up for a long time, worried about how fluid Martin's fluidity was. And about her own attraction to her confidante in her workplace. And about how everything was OK these days. And thinking that if everything was OK, then maybe nothing was OK. Eventually, she snuck in beside Martin and, suddenly angry, gave him a thump on the bum. He groaned but didn't wake.

The next morning, Martin got an email from Hilary.

Hi Martin,

You will probably be at least as unbelieving as I was about what happened me when I left the pub.

Whistling to myself, I reached the train station and saw people queuing for a train, and it turned out to be a train for Charles de Gaulle Airport. I got a ticket and sat at the back, euphoric at the serendipity of the holy and blessed day I was having, knowing that you and I could be friends, and now, here I was, on my way to spend a weekend in London with Francoise. I thought of what you quoted, 'O Lord Thou pluckiest me out' and almost made it into a prayer of thanks for my own delivery.

It was only when the train began to pull out of the station that my rucksack, with a ton of bricks in it, hit me on the skull. The explanation, Old Super Sausage Roll? Habit. I never brought a change of clothes in my former life: I just got my keepers to buy them for me. Or in the case of friends, I'd cadge them. But I couldn't expect Francoise to provide me with a change of clothes, could I? So I bought a rucksack before gong to meet her. It had two dinky little pockets and says I to myself, passport and mobile.

OH-MY-GOD I said out loud and covered my face with my hands. What's wrong? says an English woman sitting across the aisle from me, a middle aged person with a concerned demeanour. I've left my rucksack with my passport, boarding pass and phone in it at the Canadian Embassy Pub, says I. After some commiserations, she handed me her phone. Why don't you phone the Canadian Embassy? she says. I'm sure their number will come up if you Google it. So I did but they didn't answer – lunchtime, too busy. Of course I would have phoned you, but muggins couldn't remember your number, could he? Neither could I remember Francoise's number, to alert her to possible snags, so I accepted my fate and handed the phone back, with thanks, to the helpful woman. My hope was that you'd find the rucksack, which you did of course, bless you, and travelled all the way to Charles de Gaulle to drop it to the Lost Property and get it announced on the PA system. Bless you even more.

You can imagine my relief when I walked into the airport bar and shortly heard the announcement about my bag. Off I went, having drained my Martini, only to be re-directed from Lost Property to Airport Security. Once there, I was interrogated for ages because of a lotion in my bag which contained glycerol, and missed my plane. They were obviously suspicious about the manner in which the bag was delivered – assez rapidement, they said. Eventually, they let me go, having confiscated the lotion.

I felt such a complete and utter Ass. I can understand why you were in a hurry to deliver the bag, Martin, but they must have misinterpreted your haste in their state of hyper-alertness.

Anyway, all's well that ends well. I'm here in London with Francoise at last. She sends her greetings, as I do my love and xxs.

Hilary.

Martin read the email with relief, but was annoyed that Hilary appeared to be blaming him somewhat for the interrogation. Typical, he thought. Well, let's see if Francoise can change this particular leopard's spots. *Golden Ass,* he thought, *a physically beautiful person who is scatty and irresponsible.*

11

SPECULATIONS

Martin's post-Rome Diary 10 December.

I'd love to see Francoise. My guess is she's not a total stunner. Why? Well firstly, because Hilary is the stunner. Secondly, she'll be the steady one, the grounder.

Even to think of my meeting with Hilary – slender, lithe, lissom, handsome, rounded in the right places, bouncy in the right places, with the radiance of youth and its sex appeal, but above all with that *je ne sais pas quoi*, that X-factor chemistry – puts my head in a spin.

I have been trying, subversively, to get across to my students the conviction I hold that they may write all the mark-gaining analytic things they know about a poem, and still be as far as ever from *getting it, experiencing its power*. The same applies to my experience of Hilary.

On the other hand, Hilary can be perfectly ordinary and banal a lot of the time, even bloody boring. This can also apply to a poem, when you're not in the mood for it. I must use this analogy next week with my students: they will surely snap out of their *ennui* at the mention of relationships.

Among the *Disputed Questions* aired on my Medieval Philosophy Course was the issue of whether Beauty was a 'Transcendental', i.e. a quality that universally applies to all existent beings. Truth and Goodness and Unity were generally agreed to be Transcendentals in Thomist Philosophy, but there was some disagreement about the status of Beauty.

I have a different, no doubt off-the-wall interpretation of what the term means. Take Hilary's beauty. It is Transcendent in the sense that *it transcends Hilary himself.* It is beyond him. It has nothing to do with who he is, it tells us nothing about his personality, his character, his traits or proclivities. His beauty is not a mirror of his soul; it is something contingent, accidental. Hilary looks in the mirror and sees something that is *not him*, and that is his beauty. And there's nothing underneath the facade only blood and guts and nerves, organs and bones and brains and excrement, like the springs and stuffing in a mummy.

There are people who seem to be quite unaffected by their good looks. But Hilary has not been one of these. Up to now he has been one of the narcissistic people who are *defined* by their looks, which means that he is defined by an aspect which is attached to him but does not really belong to him, but rather to the lottery of nature, the gene pool. I hope he will not revert from the transformation he seems to be currently undergoing – because, where narcissistic people are concerned, the *I* becomes identified with the beauty. To the question 'Who am I?' they answer 'I am that beautiful being in the mirror'.

Jung writes about how an individual may be *possessed* by an aspect of their personality, such as the Shadow or the Persona. He considered that being possessed by the Persona – a person's public identity, their career – was particularly dangerous, as it amounted to being dominated by something which is not part of the fundamental self. To be possessed by one's beauty, however, seems to me a more extreme case: a person becomes possessed by *precisely what they are not.*

But after all this cogitation, isn't *being loved* what makes people radiant? And *loving in return* makes them even more radiant. Love is more beautiful than Beauty, and that's what was different about Hilary this time, that's why I found him even more attractive. He was not only being loved, but loving in return. He had found a True Love, and Old Misery-Guts inside me was jealous that I wasn't it.

I shudder when I realise that I, too, was a person possessed by my looks. Not only *was*, but capable of regressing, at least for another few years, by which time I will seriously be beginning to sag.

I am anxious about the further chat Sarah mentioned as I went to bed last night. *Least said, soonest mended*, I think, might be a better strategy for a while.

(Later) I asked Sarah to postpone the post-mortem and she said it could wait. 'Why don't you go and have a chat with Rónán?' she suggested. 'You haven't met him for ages.'

12

At Bofinger's

Martin was dining at the Bofinger Brasserie in the Bastille Arrondissement with his old friend Rónán, an Irish-language poet who lived in Paris. They had consumed starters of oysters and a bottle of wine, and awaited the entrée and more wine. A squad of waiters were moving to and fro, taking orders and removing platefuls of empty crustacean and bivalve shells. Seated under a magnificent dome window of stained glass, Martin was giving his fellow diner a loquacious resumé of his monastic temptations.

'I woke up standing in my monastery cubicle, naked, and lo and behold – stuck up my bum was a wooden clothes hanger.'

'Oh dear,' tittered the poet. 'Perhaps this is not the time for a rectal anecdote. I'm sure you wouldn't want me to lose my appetite, *a chara dhíl.*'

'I'm sorry, Rónán. I just wanted to say that the coat hanger was a symbolic sign of sacrilege by a consecrated monk. It seemed to me that as I stood there in the middle of the night, part of me was desecrating my vow of chastity, rebelling against sanctity. When I reflected on it later, I felt that I was surrendering to a forbidden power, to an erotic act of violation by an invisible Master, and that I was swooning under the pull of his power.'

'But it was only a coat hanger,' Rónán laughed. 'It's probably explainable by the rebellion of your erotic self against the rigours of a harsh monastic discipline. Your Eros is thrashing around in the middle of the night, when you're asleep and not in conscious control, seeking some way of expressing itself.'

'It was in the monastery that I also developed an internal orgasm,' Martin said.

'A *what*?'

'A silent orgasm in which there is an erection but no spilling of seed.'

'I don't believe it.'

'It's true, Rónán. I've had several. My orgasms aren't always like that but lots of them are. It mostly happens when I dream that something or other, usually a dark winged creature or a restless ghost, is frottaging me. The silence and lack of emission are quite convenient seeing that I sleep with my wife. On one occasion the orgasm was so intense that I actually thanked my incubus, who seemed to roll off me and lie, all passion spent, between me and Sarah.'

'What kind of creature are you?' Rónán asked, concerned about his friend's sanity.

'I'm a half-baked angel, Rónán.'

'Well I've got to hand it to you, *a Mháirtín*, your imagination has an uncanny ability to spice up your onanistic interludes.'

'In the monastery, my confessor told me I was being obsessed by a demon into using my bum, exit as it is for foul matter, to insult the sacredness of my calling.'

Ronán struggled between nausea and mirth. 'And what do you think now?'

'The jury is out. Now that my fling with Hilary has been nipped in the bud, I'm worried that the Wheel of Torture may turn around again to transgressive victimhood and steamy fantasies of bondage, canings and sacrificial rituals.'

'Better to admire Beauty, I should think.'

'Definitely. You know Edgar Allan Poe's poem, 'To Helen', in which he described beauty as homecoming for a weary wanderer? To find someone beautiful to live with is a sanctuary against ghouls and goblins. On the other hand, love is better than beauty, if there's a clash. Love is more beautiful than beauty. In the long run, of course. In other words, to find someone to live with in mutual love is a sanctuary against goblins and ghouls. '

'The long run can be a bit tedious, of course.'

Martin laughed. 'Fuck it, yes, it can be. I wrote something about Hilary and Sarah shortly after leaving Rome. Would you mind having a look at it?'

'*Cinnte agus Fáilte, a Mháirtín.* Send it on to me.'

'It's quite short, I have it here.'

'*Ar aghaidh leat, mar sin.*'

'It's a prose poem… I think.' Martin produced a sheet of paper from his jacket's inside pocket, unfolded it a little shakily, and began to read:

'*Never, now, will you ride your sleekit horse to Pingdom Come. It was like when you've been listening for twenty years and in the end you begin to hear what a person is saying to you, the voice of the person inside, and how it belongs to you and why you chose her though you didn't know why you stuck with her. Or why she stuck with you. There was something that held you in her voice, in her comportment – the way she held herself held you, the still small voice insistent over all.*'

'May I see it?'

Martin handed over the sheet of paper. 'And please, Rónán, don't say it's interesting.'

'Of course not, Martin. Interesting is a bit like the long run, isn't it? It's tedious…. But what's this *Pingdom Come*? It's not a typo, is it?'

'It's a pun. *Ping* is Hilary's word for anal intercourse. In his lexicon, to ping is to perform an act of sodomy.'

'Oh I see. And a very good pun it is, too. The only problem is, no one will get it except Hilary. If you published it, readers would think it's a typo.'

'The thought occurred to me that they might, but I ignored it.'

'Excuse me for what I'm about to say, Martin. People who go through the extremes of a passionate relationship – as you have done – often take to poetry to express their feelings when it's over, and that can be a help. The problem is that after a while, they begin to think that they can become poets. Maybe they think *This is the door God is opening to me now that he's closed the other.* I'm just bringing this to your notice, and I'm not saying you couldn't become a poet as you approach your middle years, because I detect what they call the True Voice of Feeling in the rest of what you've written. *The way she held herself held you –* that's good. The same with *sleekit horse*: I like that too.'

The words of praise encouraged Martin to tell his friend how his Roman fling ended: how Sarah had driven to Rome with their youngest son to search for him, how she caught up with him at Termini and brought him back to Paris.

'You know, Ronán, I woke up one morning recently sensing that our relationship – Sarah's and mine – is being protected by a kind of dome. You know the way the weathermen talk of a *dome of heat* in a heatwave, but this is not a dome of scorching weather, quite the opposite, it's a dome of love, a protective dome that fixes itself over people living together who are staying the course of love, despite everything.'

'Stronger than wild horses,' Rónán muttered. And the two of them were silent for a while, looking up at the motifs of flowers and fruit on the dome window's stained glass. And when their main course arrived, they tucked in voraciously to a Casserole of Shellfish, and more wine.

13

WHAT'S MISSING AT CHRISTMAS

Martin's Post-Rome Diary 27 December.

Togetherness, that's what's missing from my previous analysis, as I've discovered, considering that Sarah has now done a bunk, over Christmas for maximum effect, with Mikey and her office pal, on a skiing trip to Piedmont. Shauna will be in the same resort, too, but with a group from her school. And I'm left with Jim who's never at home except when in bed, out with his pals every night on the Christmas tear.

And I miss Sarah so much that when I met Hilary again, on his way to London, I was so lonely I hardly noticed his allure. Something is deep inside me for Sarah that cannot be dislodged: the togetherness of a couple is like that, it may be mute and inchoate but binds so tight! The holy cords that mutely bind cannot be easily bitten in twain by smiling rogues like rats. Not that Hilary was a rat, far from it, he was only trying to find himself the time I met him in Rome.

So I wrote a thesis on Beauty for my MA, eh? And forgot to mention honesty and goodness and where they fit into the equation. *No spring nor summer beauty hath such grace/ As I have seen in one autumnal face.*

Why is goodness so unbeautiful? St Francis kissing a leper, an old couple sitting looking at one another, run out of anything to say except 'Ah now, Dan' or 'Ah now, Anne' when the other finds it all too much and cries or rages inconsolably. And is it the rain or the fridge that's making that low murmuring noise?

But hark the door is opening and is it my Sarah coming back to me? It's Jim, of course, back home drunk and stumbling up to bed all the Twelve days of Christmas.

Night, Dad! Clump, clump, clump.

She hasn't phoned me and hasn't answered my calls. Teaching me a lesson, fair play to her. Driven me to drown my sorrows.

28 December

I have a date with myself tonight. I hope it will go well. I hope to find me in bed with myself before the night is through. I wonder what I should wear to allure and capture me, what kind of good time to show myself. Will I take myself to the cinema and afterwards to a restaurant? Where and when will I make a move? And what kind of response will I get from myself when I do?

Who knows? With a bit of luck I might end up in a threesome of Me, Myself and I.

On the afternoon of New Year's Day, Martin received an email from Sarah.

Happy New Year, Martin! I'll be back soon, but I have to let you know that Ella and I have become an item. I don't think it will last but I don't think it behoves you to cast aspersions either. And I'm sure you won't. A few nights ago, when Shauna and Mikey had gone to bed, exhausted from their day's skiing, Ella and I remained in the bar of the hotel, chatting till late, ringing in the New Year with some friendly English skiers. Going up the stairs together, both of us a bit wobbly, she turned and kissed me. Like that knight in armour and the lady on the winding stair in Ireland's favourite painting. I was taken by surprise, of course, but my lips weren't. The seconds went by and my mouth, of its own accord, was still attached to hers. I don't know how the kiss ended, but I found myself in bed with her. I slept with her that night and the following night, and now she's gone, just left half an hour ago, and this feeling of delight still suffuses me,

spreading over me from top to toe.
    It's been a long time, Martin. See you sometime tomorrow.
    Sarah

Sarah duly returned from Piedmont with Mikey. (Shauna was returning later with her school group.) Martin had a cold supper prepared and Mikey was sent to the local supermarket for chips, to get him out of the way. Sarah's luggage was still in the hallway and there was awkwardness and a prolonged period of silence: expectation of something more portentous than polite munching of Martin's Cesar Salad and Prawn Risotto. Sarah spoke first.

'Martin, I'm just saying: it was you who gave me permission to experience my lesbian side through your own behaviour. Believe me, my fling with Ella was not a matter of revenge. Your fling with Hilary was just the catalyst. And your clandestine meeting with him in Porte Maillot. If he hadn't been such a goof, you probably wouldn't have told me. There's a really sneaky side to you, you know.'

'I'm sorry, Sarah. Something must have happened to me sometime.'

'Don't be flippant, Martin.'

'I'm just being silly. That was Joseph Heller, actually. It's the tension. And it's not as if *you* weren't sneaky, planning that Christmas skiing trip.'

'I didn't really plan it as revenge though. Ella suggested it, and I went along with it.'

'So what do we do now?'

Sarah suddenly tittered.

'I'm glad you're amused, Sarah. Share it with me, please.'

'I often talked about you with Ella, Martin. We came to refer to you as PTFL – *Pas Toute a Fait La*. Not Fully There. She'd say to me *And how's old PTFL?* Oh I don't mean insane, Martin. Just the way you are – with a tenuous hold on reality. When I'm not fuming about your vagueness, that's actually what I like, and still like, about you. You're so wooly. Who'd want a tight grip on reality anyway?'

'So what do we do now?'

'Have you any proposal, Martin? What would *you* like to happen?'

'I think we should continue on as before. We *are* good friends, after all. We have become good friends.'

'That suits me fine Martin. As long as you let me continue my little liaison with Ella until it peters out.'

'Yes, well of course, but…'

'As I said in my email, it's not going to last. Trust me, I won't *let* it last. And I don't think she will either. But I just want to experience that side of me before I go all po-faced suburban wife civil servant blue stocking arty person again. At least *you* won't have to travel to Rome if you think it's time to put a stop to it.'

'The shock I got when I saw you face to face with me in Termini Station. I'll never forget it. So brave of you.'

'I was thinking of our beautiful children, Martin. And I was livid with you, of course.'

'And you took the Route Napoleon. It was very daredevil of you, but why?'

'I was thinking of maybe staying a night at a campsite. For Mikey's sake. But I could have driven over a cliff.'

'Thank God you didn't, Sarah. Shall we say all's well that ends well so?'

'Yes. By the way, I'm going out with Ella tonight to see a modern version of Moliere's *Dom Juan*. A trifle ironic, don't you think?'

Just then Mikey came charging though the living room door and tripped on the rug.

'Mikey, you idiot! Are you OK?'

'Sorry, Dad.' And Mikey collected a few spilt chips and went bounding up the stairs to his room, chanting 'Hup! Hup! Hup! Hup!'

'You will be coming home after the play, won't you?' Martin asked.

'Of course. I'll be discreet.'

The idea had occurred to Martin that Sarah might have made up her fling with Ella. At this stage he considered it purely wishful, and yet it brought him back to her claim that the Parisian Police were looking for him, so he asked:

'There's just one thing I'd like to know. Is it true that the gendarmerie were looking for me, as you claimed on the phone a month or so ago?'

'No, Martin. I was just being lonely and vindictive. I made it up.'

'Do you make things up very often?'

'Of course not! Only when I'm angry with you.'

'Ah so!' said Martin, injecting as much portentousness as he could into the two syllables.

'Ah so, indeed,' Sarah responded neutrally. 'But I must get ready for the theatre.'

Don't push it, Lad warned Martin's Alter Ego.

That night, Martin found it hard to sleep. It was past midnight, and Sarah had not yet come to bed. He was disturbed by images of Sarah and her office colleague making love. He didn't at all like the images, and began to fantasize about Hilary instead, of taking him to a toilet cubicle in Porte Maillot, and given him his just deserts. A pity he had already got his just deserts with the Analectomy or whatever it was called.

He took a sleeping tablet and slowly dozed off. The next thing he remembered was Sarah, returning from her date, thumping him to make room for her in the bed.

15

CHRISTY AND HILARY

The morning after he had come naked into his bed, Hilary shared some of his past with Christy.

'I remember when I was in the Order of the Spirit of God, I was very needy and didn't know what I was so needy about. Hungry for affection, hungry to be touched..... I remember reaching out and clutching the Superior's arm when for once he said something kind to me, but he drew his arm away very quickly, and I felt *soooo* embarrassed Christy, because it was after Compline and all the others were filing out of the choir. It wouldn't have been lost on them.

'I can see now that I was *la belle dame sans merci*, going around creating disturbance in the eyes of those who knew a good shape when they saw one, who could infer a shapely body even through the shapeless folds of a religious habit. And in summer down at the swimming pool having a swim, I could see that they were glancing at my body as I came in and out of the water. I wasn't conscious of my effect, though – that it gave me power over others. Above all, I was unaware that I wanted my body to create havoc.'

'Well you certainly haven't created havoc in me,' said Christy.

'Good for you, Christy. Just give me time. I remember once, at home with my parents on holidays, I went and bought a pair of jeans that were too tight for me, and a most inappropriate colour for a trainee monk - purple. Well, it wasn't that I wanted to be a bishop, the choice of purple, was it? Even though I was a theology student in a monastery, and some of the monks had actually been made bishops in foreign missionary places, I can see now that expressing symbolically the desire to be a bishop was far from my subconscious intentions when I bought the purple jeans

'We were expected to wear the holy habit at all times, according to the rules of the Holy Founder, but in those days we were reading Hans Kung and Karl Rahner, and getting mildly bolshy, changing the dress-code for certain activities such as manual work and for going places on half-days where we weren't supposed to go, like into the city where the Troubles were in full swing, to see the petrol bombs and rocks being thrown at the soldiers and for charitable visits to Catholic widows whose husbands had been killed. We had met these widows in the monastery shop when they visited on weekend afternoons to buy rosary beads, prayer books, holy ornaments and the like.

'Once when I visited a widow in the city, I met the widow's daughter, who brought me up to her bedroom to show me a secret. I half-fancied the daughter and I wondered what she was going to show me. The secret was an Armalite Rifle, which one of the rebels had asked her to hide. I was a bit disappointed, but I wasn't shocked because I'd read Camillo Torres, and occasionally fantasized about being a revolutionary priest. I was rather proud that the girl trusted me enough to show me a clandestine weapon. As it turned out, she had earmarked me as the priest she would like to officiate at her wedding. Not that she was about to get married or that I was about to become a priest. And if she ever did try to contact me to ask would I do the honours, I had probably left the order by that time.

'You mentioned once, Christy, that I had a Marylin Monroe figure. I must have had it in spades at that time. My shape became evident when I wore those tight-fitting jeans, and the colour accentuated the proposition further; not that I was aware of a proposition in the tightness and hue of my attire at all, and I couldn't understand why some of the other theology students were sniggering behind my back when I appeared among them for manual labour in those new tight-fitting purple jeans.

'Things were getting quite lax in the monastery, what with the students chatting late into the night over cocoa, wearing jeans and T-shirts instead of a tatty old habit for physical work, and going AWOL to visit the widows of the slain. Some hardline monks were saying 'the worldly spirit' was slipping in and taking up strategic positions in the house of humility and chastity, biding its time.

'The Father Superior up there wasn't as vigilant as the one who wouldn't respond to my hand-clutch, even less so since his encounter with the rebels.

'Didn't a helicopter land one summer's day in the monastery grounds? The Superior walked down to investigate this bizarre occurrence, and was confronted by several armed men in balaclavas. They had hijacked the helicopter from the army for reasons best known to themselves. It was all over the papers. One of the men pointed an Armalite at the Superior and told him to get the fuck back into his priory. After the incident, the Superior seemed to lose his zest for patrolling, whether within or outside the cloister. And this encouraged further laxity among the theology students.'

'So ye all began ridin' one another and the widows of the victims?'

'Oh don't be silly,' said Hilary, jumping out of bed and searching for his clothes. 'But there was one little brother who received a bit of erotic attention and as a result got very out of hand.'

'And that was none other than my little Hilary Golden Ass. Aww, shucks!'

'Just wait till you hear the rest. Have to catch a plane.'

'I look forward with great interest. When may I expect the pleasure?'

'I have to tie up some business back in Rome. See you sometime next week.'

16

HILARY AND DANIEL

Hilary had been delegated to assist Brother Daniel, the farm manager, as his summer assignment of manual work. This was in accordance with the order's ethos, which put great store on the importance of manual work in the spiritual development of theology students. It didn't matter whether you were *any good* at manual work; the more difficult and repugnant you found it, the better it was for your ratings on humility, obedience and penance. It was also good for your humility that your boss was an uneducated lay brother and you were a student priest.

Brother Daniel was a middle-aged, dogged sort of monk who didn't suffer fools gladly, but he took a great shine to Hilary. This had everything to do with the tight-fitting jeans and sleeveless shirt that Hilary wore in the course of his manual duties. At first, the old-timer chided him for departing from the monastery rule that the habit should be worn at all times. Brother Daniel himself wore an old ragged working habit and under it a penitential hairshirt.

As the days passed, the older monk paused more and more frequently to look, with a glint of happiness in his eye, at Hilary's body as it toiled vaguely and erratically at some bucolic task. More and more frequently, the farm brother left his own task to go to Hilary with some advice, for example to show him how to attach the milking machine securely to a cow's teat, finding an opportunity to touch his comely helper as he spoke into his ear: a squeezing of the bare upper arm, a lingering hand on the bottom!

Brother Daniel began to confess things to Hilary, indirect admissions of how smitten he was. Every morning, he said, he woke with a new feeling of happiness, knowing that Brother Hilary would be spending the afternoon with him on the farm. He confessed that he didn't want the summer to come to an end, when theology classes would begin again.

He forgave Hilary his incompetence, turned a blind eye to it, rationalized it by saying that he would learn from his mistakes.

'I was always leaving doors open,' Hilary confessed to Christy. 'The door of the byre, and the cows broke into the grain store and got at the barley and nearly died. The door of the greenhouse, and the cows got in and trampled the tomatoes. And finally, I left the door of my body open to Brother Daniel.'

For a while, Hilary resists Brother Daniel's attentions, the ever more frequent touchings and gropings.

'Get on with your work, Brother,' he says in his clipped, terse way. 'You know it's a mortal sin to be doing that.'

Even the precise, formal manner of Hilary's speech inflames the old timer, who is by now beyond recovery. He pins Hilary against the wall of the byre, fumbling at the rivet of the episcopally-tinted jeans, tries to plant his lips on his assistant's averted face.

'Give us a kiss, Brother Hilary. Ah do. Give us a kiss.'

'No. Please leave me alone, Brother, or I'll tell the Father Superior.'

Brother Daniel's lips find Hilary's, and Hilary experiences an inexplicable pleasure. His lips respond a little of their own accord. Several seconds pass before he pulls his mouth away from the mouth of his persistent suitor.

'Will you just leave me alone!' he shouts and shoves Brother Daniel away. He runs back to the monastery, his mind reeling in confusion.

He has yielded to a kiss from Brother Daniel, and a dark pleasure suffuses his body, though his mind is racked with guilt. Next morning he wakes with the memory of his response to the lay brother's kiss foremost in his mind, the taste of it still on his lips, and his entire body still experiencing the thrill of it.

The kiss meant someone hungered for him, and he had responded, not because he hungered for the other but because he wanted to be hungered for. And if there was one who hungered for him, there were probably many others who would, and at that moment Hilary knew he was born to arouse hunger among men.

17

FATHER BARK

Eventually, word got around the monastery that Brother Daniel and Brother Hilary were an item. They had become almost inseparable, and there were rumours that Brother Daniel had been seen leaving his young lover's bedroom late at night. Crude jokes were exchanged among the more knowing theology students. Hearsay had even spread to the nearby village, where there were excited whispers about 'two monks in heat', who were 'at it hot and heavy'. The rumours reached the ears of Father Bark, the Spiritual Director of the theology students. He summoned Hilary to his office.

Father Bark was so nicknamed because he had a cough that sounded like a dog's bark. An inveterate smoker, he was tall and thin, with slender nicotine-stained fingers and a goatee beard which he was constantly stroking and tugging.

He sat behind his desk, stroking his beard. Brother Hilary sat in front of him.

'Brother Hilary, I want you to be honest. Is there something…. something unsavoury you ought to tell me? There have been very unsavoury rumours circulating which concern you and Brother Daniel. Is there any truth in them?'

'Yes, Father.'

Bark froze in shock. He discerned a tone of arrogance in the theology student's voice, which he had never noticed before, in any of his routine monthly consultations. Recovering somewhat, he tried to sound more severe.

'Brother Hilary, you know very well that particular friendships are absolutely forbidden in our holy order. And especially between students for the priesthood and lay brothers. But if it's only a case of being over friendly....'

'I have been messing around with Brother Daniel, Father.'

A silence followed during which Father Bark tugged at his goatee with both hands, as if he wanted to pull it off.

'Do you not know that sexual intercourse by a consecrated monk is not only a sin of lust but also a sin of sacrilege? That your body is a vessel consecrated to God and you have defiled it?'

'You're jumping the gun, Father. It's true that we have become an item, but there's nothing much in it, just a bit of hanky panky up at the farm. It was all a bit rough and tumble, really.'

'You know you will have to leave,' Bark whimpered.

'If you say so, Father.'

'You will have to write us a letter before you leave, requesting a dispensation. I suggest that you cite unsuitability for the celibate life as grounds for dispensation. We will process your laicization in your absence.'

'Whatever you say, Father. Can I go now?'

'Just a moment. There's something important I need to know. Was it Brother Daniel who corrupted you, when you were working with him on the farm?'

'Not at all, Father. Well, maybe he was a bit – shall we say? – insistent. But I enjoyed it. And do you know what Brother James says about me? He says I'm *as bent as a brush*. What does that mean, Father? It's not very complimentary, is it? I've discovered that I'm homosexual and that I want to be homosexual, and that's all there is to it. It's not a big deal, Father.'

Bark listened open-mouthed, then broke into another paroxysm of coughing. As he stood bent over almost double by the onset, he waved Brother Hilary out of the room.

But the Father Provincial was disinclined to let an intelligent fellow like Hilary go, and gave him a final caution, ordering him to go to their monastery in Rome and study conservative theology at the Gregorian University.

18

A RENTAL AGREEMENT

The week after his attempted seduction of Christy, Hilary was back in the squat, sitting with him at the wonky table in his room. They were having cups of black instant coffee made with water heated by the Camping Gaz stove. Hilary was doing all the talking, giving the lowdown on his entanglement with Brother Daniel and his haughty responses to his spiritual director's interrogation.

Christy hadn't slept very well for the week between their previous and present meetings, because he had been trying to come to terms with his attraction to the younger man. He would certainly have thrown him out if Hilary had come dressed as a woman that first night they slept chastely together, but he was beginning to accept that it was all right for him to be attracted to a man, finally acknowledging that men can sometimes be as beautiful, and in the same way, as women. And the possibility of having children being discounted due to his economic situation, what was the difference between sex with a lovely woman and sex with a beautiful man? Not much, really, he concluded, especially when you're living in a place like London, where anything goes and the windows do very little squinting.

'I find your narrative quite erotic,' said Christy when Hilary concluded his story. 'Nothing like a bit of the cloth thrown in to spice things up.'

'I'm surprised you're not shocked at me for a blasphemous little scallywag.'

'Nothing about you would surprise me. You should be studied by a team of psychologists.'

'I did it for revenge. Not so much on Brother Daniel as on the whole institution of the Church, that multinational corporation of Pharisees in whited sepulchres. I was like a spy enjoying the sex he was having with the enemy.'

'The church will trundle along, same as it ever did, with its cockle and its wheat. I've met one or two decent priests in London.'

'Well, at least I gave Father Bark something to think about.'

'That's for sure. And you've managed to turn me on a bit too. But I have to go and give tin whistle lessons, otherwise I'll be out of pocket for the week.'

'I'm flattered to hear you say that, Christy. Well, I'm sure Paddy has updated you on my recent history: Rent Boy in Rome, *Bunga Bunga* bum-battering, Enrico's settlement, that nice man Martin whose wife put a stop to his gallivanting…'

'Yes. I'm sorry that young one Francoise from Paris didn't work out for you. I think I might have met her on the Irish music scene. What happened?'

'Too embarrassing. Maybe I'll tell you when I know you better.'

'But why are you setting up here in London?'

'I've always wanted to give London a try, and the windfall from Enrico made it possible to come and live here in comfort. And then I met you, of course, my taciturn tin-whistle tutor.'

'And you're still struggling with that tune I taught you in Shepherd's Bush. And you've been at it for *months*. I'm beginning to think there's only one kind of flute you can toot on.'

'No need for that kind of talk, Christy. I don't find it funny any more.'

'I'm sorry, Hilly, it just came out. No offence meant.'

'All right so. But this place stinks,' said Hilary, looking around at the tat, feeling the damp, shivering.

Christy shrugged, went to the bathroom sink to spruce himself up at a fragment of mirror. When he came out, Hilary said:

'Well then, tell me. Are you going to come and be my lodger in Islington?'

'On one condition,' said Christy, sounding carefully insouciant about what he was hoping for – to live in a bit of luxury for a change.

'What condition?'

'That you apply yourself seriously to learning the tin whistle.'

'Must I?'

'You must. I would never be a scrounger. I have to feel that I'm contributing something. I would give you two lessons a week, and that'd be the sub-let sorted. *And* I have an idea, just a maybe, that we could form a band somewhere down the line. Paddy plays a mean fiddle as well as the bodhran, a friend of his plays the banjo. You could be the eye-candy tooting a flute.'

'I'd gladly learn to toot the flute if it gets me into the limelight.'

'That's settled so. I'll join you in your palatial residence in a few days. But no shirking on the whistle. I'll keep you to your promise.'

'You are my rescuer, Christy. You carry me over troubled waters to solid ground.'

'We'll see how it goes.'

They both left the squat, Hilary to his plush Islington apartment, Christy to his penny whistle lessons in Fulham.

19

BROTHER DANIEL'S DESTINY

About a year after Father Bark's interview of Hilary, Brother Daniel will enquire in a Roman monastery for his former lover, only to find he is not there, he has disappeared and the monks in the monastery know as little about his whereabouts as Brother Daniel himself.

The enquirer is no longer a monk: he has been dispensed from his vows. Early the following day, he tries to end it all by jumping into the Tiber from the Ponte Umberto, but is rescued when an ageing hippie, whose car has run out of petrol on the bridge, shouts an alert to two youths on the walkway below. The youths drag Daniel out of the river and up the steps to where the witness of his suicide attempt is watching.

The ageing hippie listens to Daniel's weeping and pities him with a mixture of genuine feeling and schadenfreude. Daniel gives him some Euro coins from his sodden pocket to get a canister of petrol at the nearest pumps, and waits for his trudging return, while the police direct traffic around the car amid a chorus of early-morning beeps.

Florrie (the ageing hippie) drives away with Daniel after cursory police interrogation, and this is the beginning of their friendship as two down-and-outs in Rome.

Each day they 'fan out' around the city, Florrie to his varied deceptions, Daniel to peripatetic beggary, hoping that one of his almsgivers will stay to hear his story.

The ex-monk always returns to the topic of his *imbroglio*

with Hilary in the duo's evening conversations, and the urban desperado, sozzled but not to be outdone, speaks of the most beautiful sight he has ever seen – a young man on the Spanish Steps, drenched to the skin, who had recently held him rapt as he sashayed past with his glittering everything.

And to close each evening's drinking under some bridge of the Tiber, Florrie will quote, in his faux-Oxford accent:

Beauty is but a flower
Which wrinkles will devour...

And Daniel will reply 'It's a hard pancake, that beauty thing. A shocking bloody pancake altogether.'

20

AND THAT'S THAT!

Martin's therapist, a Monsieur le Blanc, was a lean, sharp-eyed man who looked Martin up and down and smiled thinly at his armchair-seated client. He had an air about him of closing the circle: leaning forward, elbows resting on his desk, hands joined prayerful-like before his chin, just as he'd done a few weeks before, at their first session.

'Martin, we are finished for the present. Unexpectedly quickly. My original theory was incorrect. You are not suffering from perseveration. Your recent nocturnal disturbances simply heralded the arrival of spring. My opinion is that you will have them no longer, at least to the abnormal extent you have described, now that you have confronted them.

'You could benefit, however, by having a therapy session with Hilary himself. You may have much of value to share with one another.'

'To continue our friendship, you mean?'

'Yes. It seems to me that you both need to regard one another as persons in all different aspects. Holistically. And not just as means to fulfil your sexual, vanity or rescue needs.'

'But I will still find him attractive.'

'It is a risk, Martin. Beauty is the wild card in relationships. What you have called *the most beautiful and disturbing period of your life* may develop from being a romantic illusion. The two of you would benefit from taking the risk, I feel, in terms of personal growth. And please come back to me *se les choses non passent bien.*'

118

Martin returned home elated, so much so that he blurted M. le Blanc's advice to Sarah. Her response was not the sympathetic one he had anticipated.

'Martin, if you contact Hilary once more, even on the phone, I will divorce you.'

'But Sarah…'

'I'm serious Martin. Not that I've gone all conservative, but when two people have a lot of previous, like us, it's different. I want us both to settle back, bring up our children and enjoy the innocent side of life, all those bits that don't come with such heavy chains attached. We've both had our flings and it's time to move on. *Capisce?*'

'You're probably right there, Sarah. Forget the shrink's advice.'

'I am usually right, Martin. My problem has been lack of conviction.'

'OK so. That's that…. What's for dinner?'

'Humble pie, I'm afraid.'

'I'll go for a Pizza, then.'

'Do. Get two large ones and some salads. We'll eat together as a family. Just for once.'

'But you're continuing to see Ella every day at work,' Martin complained during an ad-break in a TV serial the couple were watching later that evening. The resentment had been bothering him since Sarah pronounced her *fatwa* on Hilary.

'*Au contraire*, Martin, I have requested, and just been granted, a change of desk. As things turned out, it was for the best.'

'Was it…. .difficult?'

Sarah didn't answer, but mid-way through the next part of the drama, she reached out and clasped Martin's hand. He caressed her wrist with his thumb while his mouth shaped over and over, silently and thankfully, a single Greek word: *Ithaca*.

Quotes and Allusions:

'Awakened within a dream,
I fall into my own arms.
… What kept you so long?'
Lou Hartman, from the anthology *Essential Zen*, Kabuki Tanahashi et al, Castle Books/ Harper Collins, 1994.

Haiku 17 'Voices in the reeds…' etc., from *Basho The Complete Haiku of Matsuo Basho,* Andrew Fitzsimons (Ed), University of California Press, 2022.

'Something must have happened to me sometime.' From Joseph Heller, *Something Happened,* Simon & Schuster, 1997.

'the roses/ Had the look of flowers that are looked at' T.S. Eliot, *Four Quartets.*

Martin's remark about Ann Hathaway's seeing the kisses of other women on Shakespeare: viz. the novel *Hamnet* by Maggie O'Farrell, Tinder Press, 2020.

'Eros agape at Agape'. This is a line from a poem I read in a poetry magazine which I haven't been able to recover.

'The holy cords that mutely bind…. smiling rogues like rats': viz. Kent's diatribe, Shakespeare, *King Lear*, Act 2, Scene 2.

'No spring nor summer beauty hath such grace/ As I have seen in one autumnal face', John Donne, *Elegy IX.*

"Me, Myself and I" refers to a song of that name by De La Soul, an American hip hop trio, released in April 1989 as a single from their debut studio album, *3 Feet High and Rising* (1989).

ABOUT THE LIMERICK WRITERS' CENTRE

The Limerick Writers' Centre, now based at The Umbrella Project, 78 O'Connell Street in Limerick City, is a non-profit organisation established in 2008 and is one of the most active literary organisations in the country. We endeavour to bring ideas about books, literature and writing to as wide an audience as possible, and especially to people who do not feel comfortable in the more traditional arts/literature venues and settings.

At the Centre we share a belief that writing and publishing should be made both available and accessible to all; we encourage everyone to engage actively with the city's literary community. We actively encourage all writers and aspiring writers, including those who write for pleasure, for poetic expression, for healing, for personal growth, for insight or just to inform.

Over the years, we have produced a broad range of writing, including poetry, history, memoir and general prose. Through our readings, workshops and writer groups, our aim is to spread a consciousness of literature. Through public performances we bring together groups of people who value literature, and we provide them with a space for expression.

We are, importantly, also dedicated to publishing short run, high quality produced titles that are accessible to readers. At our monthly public reading the 'On the Nail' Literary Gathering, we provide an opportunity for those writers to read their work in public and get valuable feedback.

The centre can be contacted through its website:
www.limerickwriterscentre.com